Storm Warrior

CURSE OF THE ARCHANGELS

JAYLEE AUSTIN

Contents

The Sarim Curse

The Curse

Yahweh and Diablo once ruled in harmony, Yahweh over the spiritual part of the universe and Diablo over the physical aspect of it. However, a rebellion by Diablo sparked a war between Yahweh's loyal angels and Diablo's demons. Lucifer disagreed with the separation of power and led his supporters in defiance of Yahweh's rule.

The angelic wars caused great losses for Yahweh, including the departure of his beloved wife to live within the mortal realm. He cursed five of his sons for fighting alongside Lucifer. As punishment, he exiled their females away from Kumuria to live among the fae domains.

The protection of their archeia was of utmost importance. So, the powerful Fates scattered the precious chakra stones of the kundalini dragon, which represented all living beings. Today,

humanity struggles to maintain a delicate balance between feminine and masculine energies.

To break this curse, each chosen prince must embark on a journey to recover the scattered chakra stones of their beloved archeia's soul and undo the destructive damage caused by Yahweh's curse. It is only after they have accomplished this quest that we can hope for harmony and balance in our world.

As time flew by, the memory of the curse sank into oblivion. But fate had something else in store; a mysterious force appeared from the shadows aiming to overpower all realms. Thankfully, the Sarim Archangel Princes, who could stop the endless darkness, still held the power to save the universe.

To reach this goal, they must first find their soulmates, the archeia, and unite their spirits, so they can defeat the malicious entities. Time is running out, and the future of the mortal realm hangs in the balance, resting on the prince's shoulders. It is essential that all five succeed; if even one fails, it could mean disaster for humanity for thousands of years. Plus the true death of the archangel's soul.

Chapter One

ANANIEL CONNOR

OCEANIA, TRAINING GUILD FOR
THE NEPHILIM GUARDIANS

I stalked the rim of the translucent dome, eyes fixed on the Archipelago River's swirling currents and the row of dormant portal chutes that funneled travelers into the planet's myriad dimensions. Not a single gate bore watchful eyes. My jaw clenched at the negligence of my senior cadets. They were once sharp, now as listless as driftwood. They'd forgotten fear of divine retribution, and the possibility of a hostile race slipping through.

I raised my trident and glared at the churning storm wave beyond the tubular vents leading skyward to the mortal realm. My grip tightened around the shaft. "Gavin, report. Where is chute-nine's sentries?" I barked into my ultra-wave phone, determined not to let this dereliction of duty drag my mood any deeper into gloom.

A chuckle hissed through the receiver. "They're awaiting the new arrivals from the surface, sir. Word is, the females just came through."

"Females?" I snarled. My teeth ground together. "And our young lads can't tear their eyes away from them long enough to man their posts?" My frustration flared. The cadets' contraband fascination threatened our entire operation.

Without hesitation, I folded space around me and reappeared on

Archipelago's eastern dock, right among the slack-jawed cadets and their reprimanding squad leader. Eyes wide, they faltered mid-salute.

The leader sputtered a greeting, but I had no ears for half-hearted respect. I planted my trident's base and summoned a swirling vortex. A miniature tornado spiraled ahead of the rusty sub as it approached the dome's outer hull. Panic blossomed on every face. Shouts echoed against steel.

The submarine slammed its hatch shut . The steel ring hissed as the seawater valves sealed, and the craft slipped beneath the waves until ordered otherwise. I allowed the whirlwind to dissipate, leaving the cadets cowering among scattered ropes and coils.

"Send word to Juna," I told Gavin. "Inform her that the new females have arrived. The lads lose an hour's pay. Have them returned to their posts immediately."

A voice teased from the ventilation shaft. "Ever forget what it's like to be young, sir? Excited about a mate?"

I grimaced and massaged my temple. Even in reprimanding others, I'd erupted too quickly. "They must understand the gravity of guarding the pantheon gates." I rubbed the knots in my neck. My rash temper was ironic. I'd scolded them for laxness, yet my fury had exploded on the docks. But these nightmares of invasion, unbidden, piled upon my mind until I feared each breath might detonate me.

A muted ping came through my comm unit. Incoming transmission at chute twelve. My heart sank. Only envoys from Father's celestial realm used that corridor. Without pausing for Gavin's confirmation, I blinked out of the docks and back to my personal quarters.

My condo's door whooshed open. It was a modest two-bedroom suite off the dome's northern wing. I strode past the kitchenette and sank into my office chair before the holo-desk. A soft glow illuminated reference feeds on submarine arrivals. I tapped in the security codes and brought up the log: in exactly twenty minutes, Gavin would dock the sub and escort the newcomers to the dormitory complex.

Seconds later, a gentle rap at the door heralded my brothers' arrival. I closed the data feed and rose.

Zadkiel filled the doorway like a sentinel carved from living oak. He was broad-shouldered, unwavering gaze. Gabriel stood just behind him, arms laden with a bakery box and a plastic carrier bag.

"Cake and Moira's fudge brownies," Gabriel announced, lips curving into that impish grin that used to drive me mad. Moira's confections were harmless, even kind. "Thank them both."

"Moira said it might brighten your storm cloud of a mood." Gabriel set the sugary gifts on the side table. He kicked off his boots and propped his feet on the round rosewood table between two leather chairs.

I cleared my throat and gestured to the seats. "Have a seat. Tell Uriel I'll collect his news in due course."

Gabriel laughed. "Your highness of the sea grudgingly accepts hospitality. How far you've fallen, brother."

I bristled, but an ache in my chest reminded me why I tolerated their jibes. My shoulders slumped as I leaned beside the towering statue of Poseidon. Its stone trident pointed at the ceiling like a challenge. The god's stern expression had sent more than one cadet into a trembling puddle of guilt. Today, I felt it watching me.

A sudden stab at my left pectoral—an old scar undercut by a fresh twinge—made me flinch. The memory of old battles, old betrayals, knifed at my concentration. I folded my arms. "So. What's this urgent business?"

Zadkiel's fist brushed the scar on his own wrist as he took a seat. His voice was grim. "The next of the five Sarim princes must locate his kundalini gem. They must find the orb, or we will usher in the Third Tribulation.

My heart clocked double time. "And that would be me." Sarcasm spilled out.

"Yes, Storm Warrior." Gabriel produced a tiny ivory trumpet, blew a truncated wedding march. The brassy notes ricocheted around the room. "Your archeia awaits. Your life's noble quest begins."

I ground my teeth. Nothing about this thrilled me. Since my banishment to the earthly plane, attachments had been liabilities. I pushed off the wall. "Where is this gem located?"

"In Poseidon's Castle, buried beneath the sacral carnelian scarab of the Roman dynasty," Zadkiel said. "Metatron offers you two coins. One for entry into the Olympian pantheon, one to ride the hippocampus across the sea."

I exhaled a laugh that felt hollow. "Piece of cake."

Gabriel's smile softened. "Not until you unite with your archeia."

I swallowed. Gabriel's radiance had a way of prying at my defenses. "Fine. Who is she, and where do I find her?"

Zadkiel's eyes darkened. He leaned forward. "Your archeia is Grace Isaeva—the President of the United States."

I froze. The world shifted on its axis. Grace Isaeva, mortal leader of the human realm, champion of supernatural rights. My pulse hammered. A volley of questions slammed into me. What mortal stood so tall among the divine? How could the celestial council have identified my archeia yet withheld her identity from me until now?

I bristled. "A warlock named Norman and a coven from the other-world have embedded themselves in D.C. They threaten her life within the week."

I slammed a fist into the table. "Mortals choose their own fate!"

"But because she is your archeia, you alone can save her," Zadkiel pressed, voice low. "If you fail—"

He didn't need to finish. I'd heard the whispers: If a prince rejected or failed his archeia, his curse would unravel the fragile peace among humans, shifters, angels, and mages. A domino that toppled worlds.

Guilt and rage warred in my gut. "I lack the capacity for love," I admitted. "I'm no healer."

Gabriel's expression was a benediction of light. "She needs you, and you need her." His words cut through the storm in my chest.

My phone pinged. Gavin's update: food stores in tube three. My mind wrestled between base duties and a mortal's peril. I turned back to my brothers. "Why did the council not mention Norman can replicate Grace's form? How did he breach White House security so swiftly, casting her twin into his clutches before any sentinel raised the alarm?"

My voice roared across the marble floor. Zadkiel exchanged a glance with Gabriel. They knew more than they'd told me.

"He cloaked himself in an aura imprint stolen from her public hearing," Gabriel revealed. Within seconds, he had her."

I staggered back. "Seconds? And no alarms? No trace?"

Zadkiel's lips thinned. "Sensors logged a mirror-image signature but dismissed it as a glitch."

I pressed my hand to the statue of Poseidon behind me. Its stony gaze felt reproachful. "Then our vulnerability is worse than I feared. I chastised cadets for distraction, yet here a master warlock danced through our defenses like smoke."

My voice shook. The irony stung hotter than any reprimand I'd dished out on those docks. My own impulsive fury had done nothing to ready me for this.

Brotherhood voices softened. Gabriel stepped close and placed a hand on my forearm. "Your loyalties are torn between three masters, the guild you've sworn to protect, the woman you're destined to save, and the future of our celestial lineage."

My chest heaved. "I promised to guard Archipelago. I promised to honor the gods. Yet I nearly destroyed my own base in a fit of temper over cadets' inattentiveness, while a crafted illusion slipped past every safeguard and kidnapped my archeia."

Silence pooled around us. The weight of my failures pressed me to my knees. A primal sound tore from my throat, raw and ancient as the sea itself. My body shook with the force of it, this terror for Grace mingling with the certainty that blood would soon stain the waters between worlds.

Moments later, the dome's alarm klaxon ruptured the hush. A crimson light flooded the corridor beyond. I snapped to my feet, heart pounding. "Secure the chutes. Prepare the hippocampus coins. Metatron's offer still stands."

I gripped my trident, the metal biting into my palm like a lifeline. "I will not let him vanish me into regret. I will hunt Norman through every realm, rescue Grace Isaeva, my archeia, or die trying." My words rang hard against the stone walls.

Gabriel's trumpet tune rose in a single triumphant note. Zadkiel placed a steadying hand on my shoulder. "Find the carnelian scarab. Find your heart." Then, as if drawn by a higher will, they blinked away, leaving me alone in the bright red lights.

Alone, I stared at Poseidon's statue. The god's cold eyes held the reflection of my fear, my fury, my fragile hope. I inhaled the briny air.

Somewhere in the White House, Grace Isaeva faced a fate I'd promised to avert. Somewhere beyond our sensors, Norman peeled away at the threads between worlds.

I lifted my trident in silent vow. Tomorrow, I would ride the hippocampus. Tomorrow, I will storm Olympus. And tomorrow, I would demand justice for my archeia, my human mate, the President of the United States. The sea and sky might tremble beneath me, but I would not yield.

My roar echoed long after my brothers departed. The storm within me had only begun.

Chapter Two

ANANIEL

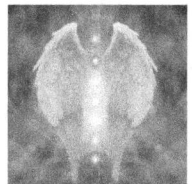

I watched the trembling images on the bank of camera monitors as two burly men heaved the President of the United States into the cavernous trunk of a black sedan that gleamed under the floodlights. My chest tightened into a vise. Disbelief crashed over me like a tidal wave. Time had never felt so sharp, so merciless. With every heartbeat I took, it seemed to steal life from Grace. Her aura dimmed, the rich violet glow draining toward twilight. She was dying by the minute.

I turned to Gavin at the console, voice low but urgent. "Gavin, program chute one to deploy at James Creek Marina. Now."

My boots thundered against the steel deck as I strode toward the ocean's edge. Salty wind whipped my hair back, stinging my face. Below me, waves roared and curled, hissing their challenge. I braced myself on the rail, then dove forward. The water swallowed me whole. Cold pressed against my skin like a living thing, and I welcomed its shock, inhaling its electric energy through every pore. The sea's power seeped into my bones, filled my lungs with purpose. I needed that surge to save her.

In the watery depths, I held my breath and willed my body to move with silent speed. Ten minutes later, my legs kicked against the surface, propelling me toward the waiting chute. A hiss of rushing air announced the chute opening twenty miles offshore. I tumbled through it, lungs roaring for breath, until I landed gently on shifting sand.

I crouched, tasting freedom and guilt both. Freedom because I could reach her; guilt because every second wasted had stolen vitality from the woman I loved. Already the skies overhead darkened. The storm clouds gathered as if the world itself sensed the urgency.

I activated my image locator, finger spinning the data dial until her position blinked red on the holo-display. I sprinted across slick grass, heedless of rocks underfoot, until I found the marina restroom tucked behind the boathouse. Its door creaked as I entered. Tile floors, buzzing fluorescent lights, the smell of bleach and stale air. Cold sweat dripped from my temples.

I pressed my palm against the door panel, flashed through the coordinates to the sedan's trunk. The metal lid snapped open under my touch, and there she lay there, pale, limp, eyes closed, beauty stolen by drugs that chilled her blood. I swallowed hard. No restraints. Physically, she was free, but her spirit was tethered to the brink of nothingness.

I eased her into my arms, cradling her like the most precious relic. My heart thundered. If a human stumbled upon us now, I could not wait. I pressed my fingers to the panic button on the chute link panel and encoded our location back to Oceania. A hiss of suction sealed us.

"Gavin," I rasped into my comm-link, voice ragged, "deploy a breathable transporter here. I'm bringing the president to Archipelago Island."

The chute's panel slid closed behind me. I lifted Grace's limp form and dashed back to the shoreline, all the while hearing the soft, terrified whisper of her fading breath. Her chest rose in tiny, tremulous heaves. I cradled her head and pressed her torso against mine. Waves broke at my feet; each one seemed to beg me to hurry.

Behind me, Zadkiel burst through the surf, carrying a human respiratory cup. Seawater dripped from his wings, arcs of silver light. Gavin arrived moments later, kneeling beside me. He placed the mask over Grace's lips, his jaw clenched. I locked her shoulders against my chest and began chest compressions in a steady rhythm: one, two, three— breathe. One, two, three—breathe. My arms burned with exertion; every pump felt like wresting her life back from the void. Finally, her eyelids fluttered. A gasp. A wheezing, shuddering breath. Relief tore through me like sunlight.

I lifted her into the ribbed comfort of the transporter pod. My muscles spasmed from the strain, but I ignored the ache. Gavin sealed the hatch and strapped her in. Then I braced myself at the pod's curved rim and, arms pumping, swam back toward the chute's opening. Once inside, I let myself be drawn along its slick interior, heart hammering against my ribs until the tube spat me out onto the landing pad of Oceania.

I yanked open the pod and carried Grace through the bustling corridors toward the infirmary. The air smelled of antiseptic and hope. Lights above hummed. "Gavin, get the healers!" I barked, my voice thick with tension.

Inside the stark metal room, Sarille and two assistants surrounded Grace's table. The monitors flashed ominously red, her vitals skirting the edge of the abyss. I laid her down gently, all at once terrified I'd broken a bone.

Sarille's hands moved over her aura, fingertips tracing unseen patterns. "What happened?" he asked, voice calm but his eyes sharp.

"Drugs," I said, tone hollow. "They injected her with something."

Lent, her guardian angel materialized in a flash of pale light. His wings shimmered with aching grief. "It was Curare," he stated, arms folded. "Enhanced with magic. It's paralyzing her muscles and severing the link between body and soul. If she separates completely, death will claim her instantly."

"Painful," I whispered, clenching my fists. A roar of disgust built in my chest. "They intend to make it excruciating."

Sarille snapped his assistant into action. "Place her on a respirator. Keep constant watch over her heartbeat. Her lungs may collapse if the drug spreads." He sank to his knees and began pressing on her chest, guiding her heart's rhythm.

Sarille looked up, worry creasing his forehead. "When was the curare injected?"

"Six hours ago." Lent's voice carried sorrow and anger in equal measure. He stood sentinel by the door, wings like wounded sails ready to guard or escort her soul to Tartarus if the worst came.

My breath came fast, each exhale a panic-laden cloud. Zadkiel grasped my shoulder, urgency shining in his eyes. "Listen," he said. "If she dies, if any of us fail, Diablo wins. The kundalini dragon's fire snuffs out, and Earth, the gods' experiment, collapses."

My stomach flipped. I thought about my mother leaving to live among humans, how our kindred spirits splintered, and how the kundalini life force fractured. If Grace died, the light of humanity, our bridge to the divine, would die. Would I be the one to end it all?

Sarille's relentless pumping jolted me back. Sweat slid down my temples. Grace's breaths were shallow, unstable. The monitors blinked every second closer to silence. I paced, helpless.

Then, a jagged idea struck. The only force I knew potent enough to wrench her soul back was bound in darkness: the demon realm. A place I'd sworn never to visit again. My gut twisted, but the pounding in my ears drowned hesitation.

I turned to Zadkiel. "Take care of her here," I said, voice thick. "I have to go."

He nodded, solemn. "Godspeed."

I strode through the hall and onto the docking bay, where chute five waited. A flash of pain seared through me as I considered how blithely I'd used flashing before, only to find out I couldn't do it underwater, or through certain wards. My power was inconsistent. I could cross realms in an instant, yet physical limits still bound me. That contradiction stung like salt. I summoned every ounce of will and flashed into chute five. In a heartbeat, I reappeared on the surface of a roiling ocean far from any mortal ship. Lightning cracked overhead; the waves leaped at me like beasts. I howled my protest across the waters, heart thundering, every atom of me vibrating with fury. The storm answered. Tornados spiraled from the winds, uprooting trees on distant shores. I realized with a jolt that my anger had given birth to this tempest. I waded onto jagged rocks, spray stinging my eyes. The city of fallen angels crouched before me, its towers black and wound with smoky arches. No subtlety remained in my approach. I let the gale come, tearing at the land, driven by a single need: to save Grace.

At the city gates, one massive chimera guarded the entrance. Its roar shook the stones. My ability to flash winked out as I stepped inside the spell-wrought perimeter, another reminder of my conflicting powers. I prepared for battle.

From the shadows strode Nuriel, angel of spell-binding. His sword glowed with runes of crimson fire. As I lunged, he murmured a ward and erected an unbreakable force field. My fist thundered against it. The metal barrier rang like a bell. Rage coiled in my chest. How dare he stand between me and Grace's salvation?

"Calm the raging storm of your temper and listen," Nuriel said, voice cold steel. His sword dissolved into a red dragon tattoo curling along his forearm.

I glared. The howling wind died in my ears. Michael's voice, soft yet insistent, pierced my thoughts. "Rafael is with her. The healers fight to keep her alive, but her spirit claws at free will. Diablo and Yahweh hold it captive between life and death, each refusing to give up the game."

I sank to my knees, heart splitting. Michael's words were a lance to the soul. "What must I do?"

"You must reach her spirit yourself. Convince her to return to her body and face her destiny."

"I can't," I choked. "I've never traveled that far beyond the flesh."

"She is your archeia," Michael urged. "You share one soul. Find her."

My jaw clenched. "How?"

Nuriel's eyes narrowed, black pinpoints drilling into me. "I offer you a binding spell. It will fuse her soul to yours, preventing it from drifting away."

An icy dread curled in my gut. The chapter of our lives had hinted at a spell both beneficial and perilous. "There has to be a catch."

"The cost is high," Nuriel warned. "She will experience every emotion you endure. She will share your internal thoughts and feelings."

His words felt like ice. Binding her might save her life, but at what price to her autonomy? To her soul's integrity? Would she want to share my life with hers?

Memories of her laughter, kindness, and light flashed as I closed my eyes. Losing her was not an option for me, and if I had to sacrifice my internal privacy to save her, the price was worth it. "I accept."

A ghost of a smile curved on Nuriel's lips. "Then it is done." He wove his hands into intricate sigils through the air. Sparks of silver magic traced ancient glyphs around us. "You owe me a favor," he added lightly.

"Name it," I said, voice rough.

He studied me. "One day I will ask you to train the nephilim, to guide them as they guard the balance between realms. Save that promise."

I nodded, though my mind reeled at the bargain. With a final incantation, Nuriel pressed his palm to my chest. I felt a ripple like lightning through water pass between us. Then, in a heartbeat, the world shifted.

Light and shadow tore open beneath my feet, and Nuriel and I fell through space into a gray dimension where tormented spirits drifted like leaves on a windless pond. The air tasted of ash and sorrow. Motes of yellow light filtered through at the edge of the fog. Somewhere in the swirling mist was Grace's fractured spirit.

Pain shot through me. Her soul's signature was fragile, incomplete and resisted like a caged bird. Nuriel kneeled and traced her outline in the air, drawing her essence into a sigil that danced in pale blue light. The binding began. Her etheric thread wound itself around my own, tendril by tendril.

"Focus," Nuriel murmured. "Dovetail your spirit with hers. Let your bond anchor her."

I reached inside, past the glass wall of separation, and offered her my warmth, my courage. I whispered her name, images of our shared memories blossoming in my mind of laughter and tears and at last she hesitated. A recognition.

Then, with a final pulse of light, the binding sealed. Her ethereal form folded into my soul-space. I felt her shock, relief, and terror all at once. A scream of triumph and anguish echoed through the gray realm.

Nuriel grasped my arm. "Return," he said, voice softer than before.

We vanished. Moments later, I staggered through the chute portal back to Oceania's docking bay, clutching a ghostly weight in my chest. I raced to the infirmary, where Rafael and my brothers kneeled around Grace's body, monitors beeping in relentless warning.

I crossed the room in two strides and pressed my hand to her still-warm forehead. "Come back to me," I whispered, desperation fissuring my voice.

Grace's soul billowed behind me. She hovered above her body, translucent and gray. My heart broke watching her tremble. I whispered in her thoughts, telling her she was safe, and to come home.

The healer stepped forward, gaze flicking to the ethereal bond connecting us. "He'll need to shield himself," Rafael warned. "That binding ties her emotions to his mind."

Pride and fear collided in me. Pride that I had saved her; fear that I had stolen a piece of her autonomy—and chained it to my fate.

I kneeled by the table and laid my palms on Grace's torso. Drawing on the residual magic from Nuriel's spell, I called the binding sigil back from my sacral chakra, sending it through her heart in a twisting, cobalt coil of energy. The room lit with a soft blue light. Grace's body shuddered, chest caving in and then blossoming into a ragged gasp. Her eyes snapped open, bright, confused, and alive.

Relief roared through me, but her first tidal wave of emotions overshadowed it, bursting into my consciousness: fear, anger, sorrow, longing. I staggered, vision blurring. Every heartbeat pulsed with her memories and fragments of pain I'd never chosen for myself.

I pressed a hand to my temple. Rafael hurried to my side with a warding barrier he draped around me. "Control it," he urged.

I gritted my teeth as her feelings settled into a dull ache, like a clawed hand still scratching inside my chest. The cost had come due. I tasted both triumph and torment. I had saved her life, but the binding stood as both boon and curse. Grace's free will was intact. She could separate and leave me, but I was forever bound to her, threatening my freedom.

I lifted her hand and held it to my cheek. She blinked at me, confusion mingling with relief in her eyes. I managed a wan smile, though my mind brimmed with her fear and hope and everything in between.

"I'm here," I whispered, voice soft. "You're safe."

Aware of the truth, I knew love could conquer death, but it came with a price no spell could erase. I was a bound man.

Chapter Three

GRACE

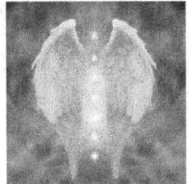

I choked on the air, sharp and harsh, as though each breath were a blade slicing through my lungs. My throat burned with a dry, suffocating agony, and I could only gape, gasping for relief that refused to come. Thirst clawed at my mind, a desperate craving for water, for any drop to soothe the raw channels of my mouth. Metal and wood pressed heavily upon me, an unyielding prison of wreckage, holding my body in a merciless grip. The horrible cacophony of screams that had rattled inside my head moments before dissolved into a mute void. Was this death? Had I slipped beyond the veil? My tears, once hot and streaming, now lay in crusted rivulets upon my cheeks, their salt stinging the dried crevices of my skin. Around me pooled a darkness so absolute it felt as if nothingness itself had chosen me for its own.

I had always pictured death as radiant, and welcoming. I'd imagined a guiding hand, a light to lead me onward. Instead, I drifted weightless in a gray fog of forgetfulness. Emotions went through me like dying stars filled with confusion, relief, and a fleeting pleasure in the absence of worry. Here, I thought, there would be no more burdens, no relentless demands upon my mind or soul. I could rest forever.

Then a jolt of pain rippled through my limbs, violent and insistent, rousing me with cruel insistence. My heart thundered at last in my chest.

Above me, faint voices echoed, disembodied and urgent. I tried to lift an arm but found myself firmly pinned. A cold, rigid mask settled over my nose and mouth, and I felt the hiss of air forced into my lungs.

We're not done yet, it insisted.

Desperation flared within me; I had to emerge from this void. I willed my fingers to move, a small protest against the darkness. A gentle, feathery pressure brushed my hand, warm and alive.

"Relax, you're in the infirmary," whispered a voice as soft as moss. It brushed against my ear like velvet. "The healers are caring for you. If you're awake, squeeze my hand."

With measured determination, I curled my fingers around the warmth of that presence, the flesh beneath my palm all too real. I tried to speak, to demand answers, but my throat remained a desert.

"Remove the air tube. She's breathing on her own."

I felt an unfamiliar freedom slide away. Then tender hands danced over my face, sending tiny tremors of energy surging beneath my skin like sparks of distant lightning. The nurse's ministrations drowned the last of the anesthesia's fog.

When my eyes finally parted, I found myself surrounded by doctors and nurses—an array of white coats, calm smiles, sympathetic gazes. Softly buzzing monitors, tubes snaking like vines, and a rhythmic beep echoing every heartbeat covered every surface in gleaming technology. I scanned each face fiercely, searching for a familiar ally. Where were my Secret Service detail, my brothers, my chief of staff? But there was no one I knew. The world dissolved into a bleak watercolor as my stomach churned with a hollow ache. Where was I?

I tried to sit, to lift myself, but pain roared through my muscles in protest. My hand shot out for the water, trembling so badly I almost knocked the cup over.

A woman in a powder-blue tunic bent beside me, placing an ice chip on my tongue. The coolness touched my scorched mouth like a blessing. "Just small sips," she murmured, checking my pulse with gentle efficiency.

As the bed backrest lifted, a tall man strode into view. He was at least six feet five, lean and perfectly proportioned, his military broad shoulders tapering into a sculpted torso. His hair, the color of ravens' wings, fell in slight disarray around a set of features chiseled so precisely they might have been carved from marble. His eyes were storm-gray, deep and intense, as though flecked with thunderclouds. With confident grace, he lifted a water cup to my lips.

"Small sips," he repeated, deep and velvety, each syllable a command and an invitation.

The sound of his voice stirred something within me I did not understand. A distant memory whispered that I should know him, and yet I could not place him. Anyone of such imposing stature would be impossible to forget, but I had never met him. Now, though, even such a realization felt frail under the weight of my current vulnerability. I obeyed, drinking slowly as relief unfurled within me.

The other healers stepped back at his silent signal—an unspoken acknowledgment of his authority. My pulse hammered in my ears. Finally, I croaked, "Where am I?"

"In the hospital," said the doctor, holding a stethoscope to my chest, as though that explained everything.

I turned my gaze back to the tall man at my side, trying to anchor myself to reality. "Do you remember what happened after your cousin's graduation?" His question fell like a stone thrown into still water, rippling with implications I dared not explore.

I nodded along as his words recited the experiences of my life. He spoke of my cousin's ceremony as though he'd been present. My cheeks burned with shame; I recalled the insidious betrayal of Norm so vividly I could taste its bitterness on my tongue. Had he been involved in this? Was he the reason I now lay here, severed from home and office? A pang of panic squeezed my heart.

"Who are you?" I demanded, anger and fear blazing through my veins. "Where the fuck was I?"

He closed his hand into a fist for a heartbeat, a gesture of disciplined strength. Then he extended his hand to me, waiting. "I am Ananiel Connor."

I stared, disbelieving. The name sounded authoritative and destined, as if fate had decided I should meet him here. My gaze darted around the room, taking in the monitors, the ventilator, the polished floors shining beneath soft lights, yet none of it felt familiar. In that moment, the realization fell on me like a thunderclap: I was the President of the United States, yet here I lay broken and alone, my entire world a thousand miles away. Why was I in this place? What political theater had brought me here?

I placed trembling fingers upon his calloused palm, and electricity surged through me, igniting my core with a heat I had never known. My heart roared in my chest like a caged beast. With sudden shame, I withdrew my hand, cheeks flaming. His gray eyes danced with the faintest hint of amusement at my reaction.

"I'm Grace Isaeva."

"I know who you are," he answered, his voice steady as a stone.

My voice cracked, and I swallowed. "Where are my Secret Service and my staff?"

"In Washington."

My world tipped. "And I'm where?"

"Oceania."

"Oceania?" My voice was small and incredulous. "I'm on the other side of the world in Australia?"

He gave the smallest twitch at the corner of his mouth. "Let's just say you're not in the United States."

I tried to taste my disbelief, but it was bitter and unwelcoming. "She needs to rest," the nurse said, adjusting an IV bag. I fought to keep my eyes open.

"Rest, Madam President. The morning hours will clarify everything."

His storm-swept gaze lingered on me for a moment before he turned and strode away. When the swelling presence of his being left my side, an emptiness settled in the space he'd occupied, as though he had taken a piece of me with him.

* * * *

I awoke again, this time to the sweet blessing of normalcy. No tubes tethered me to machines. My limbs, though sore, obeyed my will. Whatever mysterious skill the healers in that ward possessed had worked wonders. Good, because I had to go home and confront the chaos waiting for me there.

My mind went back to the day's beginning. My niece's graduation, Norm's smiling betrayal, the expressway exit into the abandoned warehouse, the sharp prick of the needle. I closed my eyes against the memory of his cruel words, the paralyzing fear as the men closed in around me. Something inside me shuddered.

Determination rose like a tide. I swung my legs over the bed and stood. The world rocked, but I planted my feet firmly and stretched, breathing in the antiseptic air. My bladder reminded me of its demands, so I sought the bathroom. Inside, I discovered a wicker basket neatly arranged with soap, toothbrush, shampoo. I slipped into the shower, letting the warm water wash away the lingering dread. It felt like a baptism, a reawakening. I emerged ready to face whatever lay beyond these walls.

Wrapped in a towel, I made for the closet. There hung the yellow sundress and sunflower hat I'd worn to Shelby's graduation, my black pumps, my clutch. Relief flooded me when I found my phone inside the purse. But the moment I tapped its screen, it stared back at me, unblinking and dead.

"Good morning," said a soft voice.

I nearly jumped out of my skin. The nurse from the infirmary stood in the doorway, a tray of garments in her hands.

"Morning," I answered curtly, still rattled.

She presented a flowered hospital gown. "Change into this, and then I'll take your vitals and bring you breakfast. After that, the healer will see you."

I frowned. Real clothes were what I wanted, not another piece of linen stitched into royalty's drab design. "Where am I exactly?"

She smiled, as though amused by my question. "Oceania." She checked my wrist once more. "We live on Archipelago Island, in the Tasman Sea."

My brow furrowed. Oceania. Archipelago Island. Part of Australia's vast ocean realm. Yet I was the President of the United States. How could I hold that office here on a remote isle? It made no sense. No matter; I needed air. "Is there a window? I need some fresh air."

"The healing ward is enclosed. There are no doors to the gardens or corridors. But I can turn on the holograph for you."

I stared. A holograph? Was this a fairy-tale land? "Any chance I could use a phone charger? Or borrow one of yours?"

"We have little need of phones on the island," she said as if naming the sun and moon. "We use our telecom system. Just place the code for your desired connection here." She motioned to the smooth tablet next to the bed. "Someone will answer."

With a shrug of disbelief, I laid my government-issue satellite phone on the circular charging pad. The nurse's words spun in my head: no need for phones. Yet my phone was up-to-date, state-of-the-art. What kind of place was this?

She clicked a sequence on the remote. The plain wall opposite me shimmered, then resolved into a rolling valley of lavender and sunflowers, swaying under an imagined breeze. The colors were so vivid, so alive, I almost believed I could step through the glassless window and walk among those blossoms. When the nurse left, the world outside my bed felt less like a prison.

I sat flipping through a magazine I spotted on the small table. People, the cover screamed, and I smirked at the absurd gossip it offered. Princess Leticia of England, scandalous photos, ignorant rumors—how petty it all seemed compared to my predicament. My heart ached with the urgent need for answers. Hidden away here in Oceania, who would even notice I was missing?

A small, sleek robot glided in on silent wheels, bearing a tray of food. I raised an eyebrow at the sight of the mechanical server. The White House could use one of these to bring me lunch. Still, I didn't trust the seafood salad it offered. I pushed it aside and set about changing into the gown. Then, shoes in hand, I inched toward the door, ready to investigate.

He was there. Standing beside the holographic garden, Ananiel Connor's presence blocked my path. My pulse leaped at the sight of him. He was so commanding, so profoundly alive. My chest tightened as an inexplicable yearning welled inside me. His hair was as dark as the ocean depths, his gaze as mercurial as storm clouds. I resisted the urge to reach out and brush my fingers through those ebony waves.

The nurse reappeared, bearing a pair of jeans, a v-neck blouse, sandals, and a small makeup bag. "Change," she said, voice kind. "Then we'll talk."

I closed my eyes for a moment. The sound of Ananiel's voice still resonated in the hollow chambers of my heart, a rich, sonorous call that stirred something buried. But I was president. I could not afford such distractions. I donned the clothes swiftly, brushed my wild curls loose around my shoulders, and squared my shoulders with renewed purpose.

When I stepped into the room again, Ananiel's lips curved in that stormy smile of his. The holographic flowers danced at his back, as though nature itself bowed to him. My senses reeled. I fought to steady my voice.

"Mr. Connor, I want to contact the American Embassy."

His eyebrow arched. "That won't be possible."

Exasperation and a sense of hopeless futility pounded in my heart, and I gripped the sheets even tighter. "Why not?"

"Because right now, the United States doesn't know you're missing."

My breath caught. The room spun. The subtle hum of the monitors, the muted palette of the ward, the ghostly wit of the flowers, it all conspired to suffocate me. Closing my eyes, a tidal wave of memory crashes into my mind.

Norm and I were back in the car, his eyes dark with hidden intent. The moment the needle slid into my arm, I remembered the cold steel burning inside me. The driver's face loomed over me, and I lay wedged between them both as their mocking voices echoed through the confined space.

"Who... are... you?" I had gasped, each word an effort as the poison spread through my veins.

He answered in a whisper of malice. "I'm a dark warlock."

I had tried to struggle, but my limbs betrayed me. "Don't fight," Norm had purred into my ear, voice soaked with power and threat. "Soon you'll open those legs, screaming for me to brand you. Once you shift and the wolf succumbs, you'll be mine, and everyone will know your secret."

I'd felt the first stirrings of the wolf within, a fierce, royal creature trapped in my blood, begging to break free. I'd clutched my mother's locket, trying to anchor myself to something real, something good. But the world had gone black, and I had succumbed.

Now the past had returned full force. I opened my eyes, breath ragged. The present was no less terrifying. I was trapped on this distant island, cut off from my nation, forced to rely on healers who spoke in whispers and technology that felt half magic.

I turned to Ananiel, voice trembling despite my will. "What is this place?"

He stepped forward, every inch of him a promise of unspoken power. "Archipelago Island is a sanctuary," he whispered, as though unveiling a secret. "A place where the ancient energies of the earth converge. We have guarded it for centuries. When your world needed a healer, the balance tipped. You came here to restore the balance."

"Me?" My voice cracked. "I'm not a healer. I'm the President of the United States."

He smiled, with an expression both tender and knowing. "Titles matter less where the world's magic converges. Here, the soul is its own authority."

I felt the sting of tears once more, but this time, neither pain nor fear. Instead, fierce determination blazed within me. If something beyond politics had chosen me, then I would have risen to that calling.

The nurse's voice called softly from the hallway, urging me to rest. I inhaled, breathing in the floral illusion of the holographic gardens and the subtle electricity of Ananiel's presence.

Chapter Four

ANANIEL

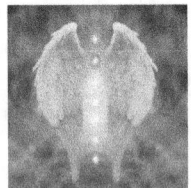

Standing inside the healing room, I saw the hologram of wildflowers blowing in the soft breeze of a spring afternoon. I'd keep that in mind, and maybe, when this was all over, I'd take her on a picnic in the wine country and make love to her in a field of poppies in the California sunshine. Grace's lovely hair made me want to touch it as I turned to her. I stared at her Cupid's bow lips and wanted to reach over and kiss that perfect mouth. A storm brewed inside me, but I suppressed the desire to claim her as my own.

"How did you know I was in danger?"

"Come with me and I'll answer your questions." She followed me out of the healing room. After signing the release papers, I took her arm. "I'm going to teleport the two of us to my living quarters." I held her close, assuming she'd come out of this slightly whirling and bewildered at the sensation of her energy cells shifting through the gravitational fields.

Inside the sitting room, I sat her on the two-seater, the floral scent of the cushions a stark contrast to my rosewood work table. Her arms clung to me, pulling me down onto the couch with her.

"That was different. My stomach's still somersaulting."

"Take a deep breath and your system will calm." I rubbed her back to soothe her.

"Well, that's one way to avoid exercise."

I rose and went to my kitchenette and brought back two glasses of water. "Here."

A circular glass window looked out onto the sea, where a school of yellow electric cichlids swam along the outer domes of the island. She moved from the couch and immediately rushed toward the window.

"We're really in an underground water city?"

"Yes." I wanted to say something sarcastic, but when she gulped a breath, and her normally pink skin turned a pale gray. I flipped the intercom button. "Jeffrey, send a tray of finger sandwiches and medicinal tea to my quarters. Pronto."

Jeffrey served as the guild's organizer, handling everything from meal preparation to making sure the Nephilim guardians didn't get into too much mischief terrorizing the cadets stationed to protect the portals.

"Come back from the window and gather yourself." Her dazed look concerned me, but she raised her hand to prevent me from approaching any closer and took one chair.

I understood her need to process where she was and what had happened since her arrival.

She clenched her fists. "Where is Archipelago Island, exactly?"

"The land doesn't exist in your realm. It belongs to the celestials."

"Whoa, angel. I'm where?"

"Below the sea, in a safe place where hybrid angelic children train to exist in your realm."

Alarm came into her eyes, darkening to a shamrock green. Her chin quivered as she swallowed hard.

"I can't... I can't..."

"You can. Focus on the floor and put your head between your knees. Let out your breath."

I put my hand across her back. Dark strings of her aura swirled around my fingers, and I pulled her fear into my own turbulent body.

"I'm okay."

Her gaze darted around the room. "And how to we get off this island?"

"I'll show you the chutes later." I tapped a button under the table. The screen over the window closed, and a hologram garden of wildflowers appeared outside the makeshift casement. The scene deflected the claustrophobia I saw stirring in her expression. "We have healers who could help with your fears."

"What do you know of my fears? Are you also psychic?" Her body stiffened, and she moved deep into her chair.

"To bring you back from the etheric fields, Nuriel, a spellcaster angel, tied your emotions to me."

"Can you see my memories?" Her hand flew to her mouth.

"Through the spell of the sigil, I felt your panic. Your heart beat erratically, and I sensed your desperation to escape."

Ten minutes later, a tap on the door. "Enter."

Jeffrey, along with a robotic server, brought an array of cheese, crackers, and small cut cucumber and turkey sandwiches. Jeffrey took the tray and set the food on the side table against the wall. He poured her a cup of tea. "Drink this. The tea's a mixture of lemongrass and gotu kola to soothe your nerves."

"Thank you." Grace sat in one chair, placing her cup on the small round table.

"You must be the woman the others speak of. You're more elegant than they describe."

With no actual reason, I wanted to send Jeffrey, with his savvy demeanor and aristocratic good looks, from the room and keep her sheltered from the others.

Jeffrey handed me the cloth. "You've got a message from Zadkiel."

"I appreciate your urgency. I'll advise you to regard the evening meal. How are the ladies faring since their arrival?"

"Well, Sophia organized the group with her warm, motherly touch." Jeffrey left.

Grace sipped her tea and was eating the sandwich. Apparently, from the uneaten breakfast I noticed in the healing wing. She was hungry. I turned off the hologram, and the screen disappeared.

I unfolded the note written on ancient scribe cloth. *She is more than what she seems, a surprise I'm sure you'll enjoy!* The tone of my brother's words made my throat constrict.

Footsteps came up behind me as I gazed into the ocean, watching Poseidon's golden dolphins dance a pirouette. Grace's presence in my home stirred the ache in my soul. I didn't want her to return to the surface and risk her life as president. Next time, the mages might kill her. Zadkiel's exclamation rattled me; I hated unexpected events. I kept my world tidy. Every aspect ran like a finely tuned piano until a sexy dark-haired beauty came crashing into my life. I'd wanted to find my archeia, but now I wasn't so sure we were a suitable match.

"Who are you?" she asked in a deep, husky voice.

Her feathery touch on my shoulder sent shock waves to my cock.

"I'm going to tell you something most humans consider mythology or religious."

Grace gave me a double take.

"I'm listening." She stressed certain letters like she didn't know whether she thought I was a lunatic.

"Sit down, The story's quite complicated." I followed her back to the leather chairs and took a seat opposite her. "Archipelago Island is the central hub for every pantheon within this galaxy."

"When you say pantheon, do you mean like Greek and Sumerian gods?"

"Precisely." I struggled to find the proper or coherent words to explain and make her see the reality of the situation. "I'm the leader of the Grigori watchers and the Nephilim guardians. The guild serves as a training facility to teach our hybrid children to become human guardians." Bringing her to my quarters probably wasn't the best idea, but I wanted to establish a connection before the guardians became overprotective of the mortal female.

"Grigori watchers are fallen angels if my knowledge is correct, and the Nephilim are offspring from the angels' union with human women."

She made this easy when her hand rested on mine. "I'm an archangel. After the celestial wars, my brother, mother, and I went to the earthly realm. Her questioning eyes were something I wasn't ready to see. My instincts to protect and shelter her were powerful, yet a part of me didn't want to surrender and face the agony of death should I fail to fall in love with Grace. I'd found a satisfying life within the dark realms of the sea and preferred my father not to screw with his forgotten sons. I wanted no part of the Kundalini dragon and its promise.

"Why was I here?"

I wanted to tell her we were once spirit-mates. The bitch of the situation was Grace had to fall in love with me, and I her for a true mating of spirits to exist.

"For your protection. I didn't know where else to bring you. You were dying, so I brought you to my home." I turned toward her and offered her a chair. "Sit, finish your lunch, and I'll explain the dilemma in which we find ourselves."

She lifted one finely arched eyebrow and took a seat.

The pain in her eyes would haunt me forever. Someone she believed loved or at least cared for her had betrayed her. A man she allowed in her inner circle.

"How did you know I was in danger?" She nibbled one of the finger sandwiches.

"Zadkiel, my older brother, asked me to monitor you. We suspect a coven of sorcerers intends to disrupt the balance between the mortal and supernatural domains."

"Why do you care what happens to me?" She poured herself another cup of tea which by now was room temperature and sipped.

"That's an interesting story."

She narrowed her eyes and regarded me with a long, silent, sizing-up moment. "I'm listening."

"In the Celestial realm Yahweh and Diablo contend for rulership over humanity."

"Hold on a minute. You're telling me angels are competing to see who will control?" Instead of replying, it was easier to continue on since I wasn't used to having my authority questioned.

"A long time ago, a curse happened, and you're part of the story."

"Right, what turnip truck do you think I fell off of?"

"The truck that almost killed you," I snapped. "That man you consider your lover is a warlock. A dark mage with extremely dangerous powers."

Her soft pink skin paled. No doubt memories of the night replayed themselves in her mind. I pushed down my rage that the man almost succeeded in killing an archeia and condemning the twelve Sarim princes to our true death.

"Sorry, but this is quite a lot to process."

I studied her with her solemn eyes. I sniffed the air, a strange feeling of otherworld energy edging at the corners of my consciousness. Her fragrance reminded me of the earth elementals'. No, that wasn't quite right either. She appeared human, but I sensed something different. I couldn't place my finger on the nagging thought that she lived among the humans, but she herself was another species.

"We have limited time to prepare you to fight the magical elements before you must return and take back your presidency."

Her hands clasped, she twirled her thumbs drawing my gaze to her lap. "Wow!" She exhaled a long breath.

"They've used a mage capable of using transmutation to appear in your likeness."

"So, no one realizes I'm missing that's awesome." Her laughter bubbled over in a choked squeak.

"Zadkiel, mentioned your pre-arranged seclusion to mourn your parents' death works in our favor."

"How did you know about my mother and father?" Her eyebrows flying to her hairline endeared her to me.

"When Zadkiel learned of your relationship to the curse, he investigated your background."

"Everything?" she spoke the word in a breathy rush as if she hid secrets. "I can't leave my family in the dark."

"For now, you're safer if they assume you're away on vacation." I gave her a long, searching glance.

Her eyes misted with tears.

"What about the fact a murder attempt has been made on my life?"

"Irrelevant. If you want to make sure the civil rights legislation passes Congress, you'll need to stay quiet for a while longer."

"Where does that leave me?" She folded her arms under her breasts in a typical gesture of defense.

"Alive."

"Now what?"

"We prepare for the fight of our lives."

Chapter Five

GRACE

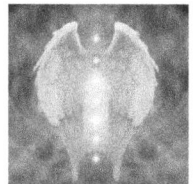

After our conversation, Ananiel led me down a candlelit corridor to the adjoining chamber. "I've prepared an assortment of garments you might find agreeable." His voice was soft, yet carried the weight of command as he opened a heavy oak door. Inside, a grand four-poster bed draped in ivory linens stood beside a carved mahogany dresser and a full-length antique mirror. On the walls danced portraits of nymphs in moonlight and gilded dolphins leaping through celestial seas.

Raised a devout Russian Orthodox Christian—forced all my life to deny my shifter heritage—I smirked at the lavish otherworldliness. Yet beneath the amusement, my heart thrilled at the reality of hidden realms: shifters, nephilim, archangels, all living alongside humans with their own councils and laws. My convictions about every species' right to exist felt vindicated.

I hesitated in the doorway. "Why two bedrooms?"

He cleared his throat, gaze flicking away. "This one is for guests. I entertain seldom, but I wanted your comfort assured. You'll stay here."

I swallowed, unease fluttering in my chest. "I can't share a room with you."

Ananiel's lips curved with amused reproach. "Then the infirmary is yours. The Grigori watchers occupy the other apartments; they know you are off-limits."

I clenched my fists to still my indignation. "Who else is on the island?"

"Four dormitories of trainees," he said. "And aside from you, one other human woman."

My brow rose. "A human?"

A ghost of sorrow darkened his eyes. "Ariel, our Dominion archangel, chose her long ago. Sophia, his wife, lives here."

"Ariel's an angel by nature," I said.

"He trains Nephilim to protect humanity," Ananiel explained, closing the distance between us. "Sophia helps acclimate them to mortal life."

"And Sophia herself?" I ventured. "What is she like?"

Ananiel's face softened. "She brings sunlight even to our island mists." He fell silent, as if recalling a joy too precious to name.

I traced the curve of his rigid jaw, resisting the urge to comfort him. Instead I murmured, "She sounds important."

He nodded once, distant. "She will seek you out soon. She chose the cherry blossom I left in your room."

I managed a polite smile. "I'll thank her."

A sudden tightness seized my chest, an instinctive horror at being trapped beneath the ocean with no escape. My pulse thundered in my ears; my wolf clawed at the walls of my mind.

Ananiel's voice was gentle but insistent. "What's wrong? Your heart races as though you're drowning."

I sank onto a small velvet sofa. "I need air. How do I get out? I feel trapped."

He kneeled before me, one hand on my back. "Breathe."

My lungs heaved. "Do you have my purse?" I searched in the dresser.

"Sophia placed it in the top drawer." He retrieved it and returned, sitting close enough that his thigh brushed mine. I dug in, drew out my Zoloft bottle, and broke into tears of relief.

"What's that?" he asked, concern sharpening in his gaze.

"Anti-anxiety medication." I swallowed hard. "Three panic attacks today. If this continues, I'll..." My voice trembled. His expression darkened. He snatched the pills from my hand. "You won't need these here. We have work to do." He tucked the bottle into his jeans pocket.

I stared at him, disbelief and anger warring within me. "Who the hell do you think you are to decide that?"

He lifted my chin. "I am the man who will keep you alive."

The words struck me like lightning. I needed those pills to hold back the fear of water, the fear of the body double impersonating me, and the fear of an abandoned life. "They help me manage the trauma."

He pressed his palms against mine, urging them face-down on his. "Tell me about your fear."

I jerked back. "Don't."

But he was already drawing me close: lips brushing my throat, heat fanning along my arms. My wolf growled, seeking release; my body trembled with a longing to yield.

"Trust me," he whispered against my skin.

The tension between us crackled. A storm of power swirled in his eyes, a glint of gold briefly igniting the smoky depths. I turned away, breathless. "I'm fine."

His lips trailed down my collarbone. "What happened?"

I felt the walls I'd built since childhood crumble. My head found his shoulder. "In Chechnya... a bomb. My parents... I was trapped under rubble for days. I survived in a bathtub." Tears slipped down my cheeks.

He held me tighter. "How old were you?"

"Thirteen."

"Give me the fear."

A tremor raced along my skin. I'd studied magic, but never felt it so tangibly. "How—?"

"Trust me." He wove a spell around us, a silken tether of crimson light linking our sigils. My terror peeled away, absorbed into him. My body went limp, like waking from a nightmare.

He cupped my cheek and kissed me. "You'll need none of those pills again," he murmured.

I lifted my head, bewildered. "What did you do?"

"I took your pain into myself."

My breath caught. "Why bind yourself to me?"

He met my eyes calmly. "Your spirit is connected to this place." You hovered between worlds. I would not let you wander lost."

My heart constricted with gratitude and a desire, a raw need to trust him. Yet reason surged up. "I must return to Washington. I have a team to alert. If witches invade D.C.—"

Ananiel rose, a silhouette against the doorway light. "In a few days, we will plan your journey home. Until then, you stay."

"I can't," I whispered fiercely. "Norman, he'll undo everything I've built."

He glanced back, expression unreadable. "He believes you're dead in a car trunk. The Dominions saw fit not to correct him."

I shivered at his words. Revealing my panic, I growled low. "If they think I'm dead, the Republicans will seize power in the house."

He met my gaze and, for a heartbeat, I saw infinite compassion and the iron will of a guardian who would brook no refusal. Then he closed the door behind him, leaving me alone with my racing heart and the glittering images of dragon light in the room.

Alone, I knew Ananiel was the man who would keep me alive. But at what cost to my heart?

Chapter Six

ANANIEL

Grace's fear coursed through my system. Every cell of my body needed to be rid of the contaminating emotion I experienced her anxiety. Inside my private quarters, I opened a personal chute located inside my shower and programmed it to open in Greece. I shot through the portal and dived deep into the sea, releasing the thread of turmoil. On the ocean's surface, I created a tidal wave that rippled through the seas of Greece, helping me regain my strength.

I flashed to Mount Parnassus, and inside, I kneeled at the Oracle in search of an answer. The sigil signature bonded Grace to me. Her psyche and emotional thoughts felt like my own, making concentration difficult.

Bright lights flashed from the Oracle, and the Greek Moerae appeared. In respect, I bent down on my knee and lowered my gaze.

The first fate of destiny spoke, "A new age will rise; go forth and pave the way."

The second fate of destiny placed a thumb on my third eye. "Go see Moira, the mother of the Kundalini. She will offer you the foresight you need to endure your next challenge."

The third fate of destiny settled a hand across the wound. "Allow her to heal your heart. The time to release the past is now."

I sighed and took my leave of the Fates. Outside the temple, I returned to my quarters, freshened up, and prepared to visit my brother's wife. Once on the surface, I flashed to the magical entrance that crossed over into Sierra Madre, a human community. Needing time to think and figure out how Moira could help me, I walked the five miles to town. Smoke exhaust from the vehicles and the noise of the crowd helped to drown out the buzzing in my head.

Grace constantly let out a low growl of discomfort, like a dull ache that registered deep inside me. In my mind, I sensed she was more than a mortal human, but of what species? Feathery Bakery was at the end of the block. I opened the door of the cafe, which was filled with the scent of cinnamon coffee.

"Ananiel." Moira's sweet voice rang with delight. "What are you doing here?" She came to the counter smelling of spiced apples and oats.

"Advice."

Her beautiful amber eyes glowed, and something appeared different. Her cheeks were fuller, and her russet hair shone with golden lights, filling the room with pure happiness.

"What's got you concerned?" She squeezed my biceps and used telepathy. *"Meet me at the house. I'll be there in fifteen minutes."*

I looked around and waited at the counter as she bagged my favorite blueberry muffins and a cup of steaming coffee. Moira was an elfin seidr goddess who married the bringer of light, my brother. Moira's magical wards protected the shop and kept out all dark energy. Her luscious potions brought in customers, where they found a haven of delight, a place of wholeness in a world full of chaos.

As I exited through the bakery, a handful of teenage boys came bustling inside, hollering out their orders for chocolate chip cookies and Moira's famous crumb cake cooked with special magical herbs. After Uriel and Moira's wedding, I enjoyed seeing how happy my brother's mate made people in the community. I walked down the alley so no one would see me, then I flashed to Sierra Madre. I wandered around the grounds, waiting for Moira to arrive. A knot formed in the pit of my stomach, and I wasn't sure how to approach my theory that Grace might be supernatural.

Moira arrived in Brigit's, her roommates, bright red convertible and waved. Uriel was one lucky son-of-a-bitch to have found his archeia. Now it was my turn, and I didn't have a clue how I'd ever make Grace fall in love with me.

I finished the last of my muffin and walked over to her car to help her unload the packaged cakes. No way could I return to Archipelago Island without a supply of her luscious treats and not hear about it from the guardians.

Moira unpacked her bags and made a pot of coffee. "What do you know of elfin shifters?" I asked, standing at the back door.

She turned, leaned against the counter holding a large piece of fudge and rolled her eyes upward in thought. "Shifters are rare in Alfheim. Most of the elfin race carry magical DNA, which contradicts the shifter DNA, making the animal dormant. Why do you ask?"

"I think Grace is an elfin wolf shifter."

Moira handed me the candy, pulled out a chair and sat at the table. "What makes you think she's elfin instead of human?"

I flipped the chair around, crossed my arms over the back, and took a seat. "Her scent doesn't smell human or shifter—it's different, a mixture of pears, cinnamon, and orchids."

"In Nordic mythology, the great silver elfin wolf appears in times of horrific distress. We won't know if she's an elfin shifter unless she tells you."

"Part of Grace's spirit was bound within me. A wolf spirit is what I feel. I sense a strong power that rivals even the gods."

"If that's the case, she's in great danger. Uriel said the warlock deliberately placed her in a comatose state. If that's true, and the covens are aware of her heritage, they'll want the power of the elfin wolf."

"That's what I thought."

"If she's the sacred silver wolf, she's alpha. A powerful leader of all the shifter packs. She won't easily submit to those weaker than herself. She'll need someone powerful to control her feral passion when she finally shifts."

Moira went to her bookcase, pulled out her animal tarot deck, and shuffled them before turning over two cards. "Her path is the dragon, the same for all five archangels and their lost archeia. The obstacle facing her is the snake. Her creative life-force is blocked. Her magic lies dormant. That is why her wolf calls to you. You must awaken her spirit and bring her wolf to the surface. Make her shift, then she'll experience her magic. She'll need you to train her to listen to your commands. As alpha, she'll want to dominate, but it's essential you make her submit."

"Why me?" Ananiel strummed his fingers through his hair unsure of what this meant. His archeia, a wolf shifter intrigued him, especially an elfin wolf shifter.

"You're her true mate and her wolf recognizes you." Moira lowered her gaze and continued to read the cards. "Nuriel's spell has bound Grace's wolf spirit to you."

"She was dying. What did you expect me to do?"

Moira chuckled. "I'm not criticizing you, just amused at your willingness to bargain. You and your brothers love to gamble and make deals."

"If she's really my archeia?" A fire shot through my body, and I grasped my chest, fighting the anguish searing my skin. Moira wiped my forehead with a cloth.

"The Kundalini Curse." She unbuttoned my shirt. "Has the cicatrix festered?"

She ran her fingers right below my left pectoral muscle, tenderly outlining the scar. "The pain grows stronger. My skin has bled."

Moira walked to the cupboard and pulled out an ointment solution from her healing herbs. "Use this to ease the discomfort."

Taking the remedy, I placed the jar into my pocket. "I'm fine."

"Ananiel, you look bewildered."

"What do I need to know to help Grace?" As leader of the Grigori Watchers, the watchers brought knowledge to mankind, but now I scrambled to understand the ways of the shifter clans.

"Because of the sigil connection, you will bear the knowledge of her sexual transformation. You will need to control her alpha, claim her as your archeia and remember wolf's mate during the lunar blood moon eclipse."

"What does that mean?" A quiver of misgivings stirred a need to abandon the kundalini obligation, return to Archipelago Island, and the Nephilim guardians I swore to protect.

"Lust, pain, and sexual orgasm will be part of bringing the sacral chakra magic to the surface."

I wasn't sure what sex had to do with shifting. But having sex with the beautiful female was something I could offer.

She put a hand over mine. "I'm making some assumptions, but if my conclusions are correct, you'll be able to help her successfully complete the transitional cycle of a female wolf."

"Gotcha."

"To open the sacral chakra, she might need more than one male. I predict she's suppressed her wolf. She hasn't allowed her mind or body to merge with the pack during the moonrise. Because of this abstinence, she's buried her elfin light deep inside her soul. She's denied the natural progression found in most wolf packs during the lunar moon festivities."

I didn't expect to hear I might have to experience her taking another male and fought back a surge of possessive anger. "If she's my true kindred archeia, I can't just let another man pleasure her."

"Aah! You have feelings for her."

I pushed the chair away and walked to the screen door. With both hands in my pockets, I let my gaze wander over the forest landscape. A couple of minutes passed before I turned around and faced Moira. "I'm a territorial man, not given to sharing what is mine."

"Mark her. Take control of the transformation. You chose who will help you during the waning crescent cycle. Once she is prepared and ready, then you must blend your souls and mark her with the trident."

"What if she objects?"

"She won't. She'll sense the bond you carry inside you." I combed my fingers through my hair and wandered around the kitchen. On top of making her fall in love with me, I had to dominate her into submission using other men. I didn't object to the thrill of watching and taking part in other circumstances, but this woman was my archeia. I walked back to the table and took my seat.

Moira picked up the animal tarot from the table and flipped a three-card spread. "The lamb." She ran her fingers over the layout and glanced out the window. "Grace has a powerful message to bring to the world.

The world needs her vision of change. She brings transformation, but at a significant cost to herself. Her past has brought her to you."

"My wrath and anger still burn deep within. How can I help her if I'm unable to truly love again?" Moira rose from the table and poured us both a cup of coffee.

As she removed her glamour and shared her natural elfin energy, her golden beauty glowed. My impatience waned during her magic. She knew how to calm my turbulent seas.

"Here, eat a brownie, and I'll hurry with my story." She flipped a second card. "Ahh, the scorpion. She is a passionate woman determined to protect those she loves. Her career is important, and she takes her job seriously. Be patient with her; she feels flustered and hides her feelings. Together, you must face your darkest pain and learn to trust each other. Only then can you heal."

"How will I make her fall in love with a broken spirit of a man?"

"That is for you to figure out." She flipped the last card—the future. The crocodile. "This card is both a warning and a gift. Protect her from herself. Many people highly desire a fae wolf. You will need to keep her in Oceania during her shift and the completion of the blood moon ritual. Her magic must fully weave and transform into the silver elfin wolf if she is to defeat the sorcerers."

"Yahweh wants her to return and take her place as president."

"That's interesting. Keep her safe. Her magic will not fully be hers until after the mating ceremony on the night of the complete lunar eclipse. Why the urgency since a double is in her place?"

"Diablo uses fae bogies instead of his own demons to create chaos and distrust within society. Since most bogies are less harmful until provoked. Many come from the dark fairies of the Unseelie clans and are willing culprits playing pranks on unsuspecting mortals. They grow stronger with the help of your necromancer brothers." A spark of sadness entered her eyes.

My shoulders tensed, realizing, "I surmise the struggle between species is only beginning. I fear the humans will pay the price for this disagreement between the gods."

I kissed the top of her head. "My brother is a fortunate man."

"Wait." She pulled out a card for me. "Crow."

I smiled. The raven shifters played an important role in the dragon's resurrection. Of course, they'd play a role in my life. "And?"

Moira arched a brow in mock amusement as she continued to read the cards. "Patience." She glanced up from the table. "Your greatest obstacle will be anger over your banishment to Earth. You must balance the three realities of the past, our present, and your future. Come to terms with the journey. I see your attraction to your archeia, but the pain of the curse hinders you from seeing the future possibility of a new way of life."

"Some wounds can't heal."

She kissed my cheek and handed me the package of sweet breads and treats. "When her transformation occurs, protect her, and shelter her. Until the moon's cycle is complete, she is vulnerable. Prepare."

Chapter Seven

GRACE

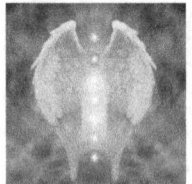

My eyes drank in the city. A living vision of opalescent towers rising from the seabed, their facets refracting sunlight into a thousand rainbows. Each crystalline spire glimmered like a city forged from liquid diamonds. Suspended walkways meandered between the towers, looping across cascades of water that seemed grown rather than built, as if the stones themselves exhaled the torrents that fell in silken sheets into lily-filled basins below. I pressed a hand to the reinforced glass of the observation tunnel, trying to still the flutter in my chest. Part of me—my wolf—chattered its delight at the sight of so much water. The rest of me, the side I presented to the world, felt something like awe.

"How do you accomplish such an effect?" I asked, turning to the guardian at my elbow. His presence was like a pillar of storm clouds, tall, broad-shouldered, and clad in robes that shimmered with an undercurrent of liquid blue. Ananiel's voice rolled out in a rich baritone that vibrated through my bones. I bit back a squeal of delight, my pulse clattering.

"The waterfalls keep the chi flowing through every avenue of the guild," he explained, his eyes bright with pride. "Our architecture is not merely ornamental. It is a conduit for mental manifestation. The

Nephilim who gather here descend from angel and human relations, guardians of the human world. For them, water is more than an element: it is their origin, their link to the divine, and the wellspring of their strength. These streams forge the bridge between the celestial and material realms, empowering students to shape reality with focused thought."

I nodded, though part of me was still fixated on the fluid beauty surrounding us. "And humans, do they know of these guardians?"

He inclined his head, with a shadow of amusement in his gaze. "Few mortals sense us. Some psychics, a handful of witches, and those rare souls attuned to the unseen. Otherwise, our guardians blend into human society. They take human spouses, raise families, and serve as teachers, healers, and beacons of hope. In the coming age, every pantheon will call upon their talents."

Heat flared along my neck. My government could use guardians in Congress instead of those self-serving morons locked in their echo chambers. I laid a hand on his arm, an almost casual gesture, but I felt my wolf stir at the contact. Ananiel's storm-gray eyes flicked down to my hand, then lifted to meet my gaze, and time lengthened.

My wolf growled softly, content. The scent of his skin reached deep into my bloodstream, uncoiling something both thrilling and danger-ous. His shoulders sloped into a narrow waist, and every taut muscle spoke of power withheld. I swallowed, feeling far too much like a schoolgirl with a crush. I forced my desire into a tighter knot.

"The United States government could benefit from trainees of your caliber," I managed, drawing a steadying breath.

Ananiel chuckled, laying his hand over my shoulders in a protective arc. Warmth bloomed where his palm rested. "Guardians avoid politics. Too messy."

His laughter, gentle and resonant, eased my tension. I let myself lean into his warmth as we continued our tour. Golden light spilled across paths lined with jade-hued moss and curling ferns, leading us to a vast complex of six dome-crowned warehouses. Between them stretched gardens draped in violet blossoms, paths of polished basalt, and tranquil pools reflecting the shifting hues of the overhead currents.

Ananiel guided me through the central arch of a dome, his palm pressed at the small of my back. My wolf rolled in delight at the subtle connection, and I closed my eyes for the slimmest moment, savoring the electric thread between us.

"Each of these buildings houses a pod of twenty students, ages twenty to twenty-five," he said. "Here, they hone physical endurance, mental discipline, and elemental mastery."

We entered the fitness pavilion, its doors parting to reveal an Olympic-sized pool illuminated by bioluminescent algae. Every swimmer I saw was over six-feet-five, their bodies sculpted as if chiseled by divine hands. Ribs of muscle curved into razor-sharp obliques, and each man's lithe waist tapered into powerful thighs. My pulse hammered in my throat. My wolf's hunger surged at the sight of such raw, unguarded strength.

I flushed and turned, cheeks burning. "I was just admiring the facili-ties," I stammered.

A laugh floated back to me. "Wait until you see the goddesses," a voice said. A woman, statuesque and muscled like a living sculpture, approached. Her skin was the richest brown; her eyes, molten pools of mahogany. She slipped her arm through mine. "I'm Sophia, matriarch of the guild and Ariel's wife. Forgive my tardiness; my little ones staged a waffle revolt this morning."

I blinked. "You have children and a husband?"

Sophia nodded, her smile warm and maternal. "I'll leave Grace in your hands for now," she told Ananiel, who ducked down a side corri-dor. "After the tour, return to my quarters." She steered me toward another dome.

"Welcome to the female pod," she said. Magnetic doors slid aside to reveal a circular chamber divided into personal alcoves. Each alcove contained a bed, a small wooden chest, and a window looking out onto the curve of the sea. In the center, six women in athletic wear formed pairs and practiced knife-defense drills. Their movements were precise, deadly, and elegant.

I felt an ache to join them, to twirl a blade in my hand and unleash pent-up aggression. "Will there be a chance to train with them?" I asked Sophia.

She smiled knowingly. "They practice every morning. Speak to Ananiel, and I'll arrange a session with our top trainers."

"How about tomorrow? I need to sharpen my knife skills."

Sophia's face sobered. "First, we must prepare you for the magic awakening within you."

A jolt of fear hissed through my spine. Had she sensed my wolf? The suppressant pills I took every morning usually smoothed out all traces of my nature. I clutched the pendant at my throat, an intricate triquetra forged from moon-silver.

My mother's stern warning: Don't let anyone discover your true identity. I kept my tone light. "What magic?" Sophia's gaze pierced me. "You are an Elfin Wolf—an extraordinary rarity. Shifter and Elfin blood seldom mingle, yet both run in your veins. I sense the medicine you used to shield your true form."

My stomach twisted. I should have denied it. Instead, I slipped back into my practiced persona. "You're mistaken. I work closely with the supernatural community."

She closed the pod door behind me, stepping forward until the hush of the room cocooned us. "Although you claim to work with us, you hide your heritage." She stared at me, putting her elbow on her hip, waiting... "You hide your magic as though your life depends on it."

Anger burned up my throat. How could she be so bold? "I was born in the shifter community of Georgetown, right on Capitol Hill. Hardly un-American."

She raised a careful hand. "Claws in, Senator. I stand with you."

Shame pricked me, but I forced a laugh. I wanted nothing more than to slip back to my office, to the security of familiar halls and cold logic. I fingered my locket, the only proof I had of the hidden world. Sophia's next words cut straight to my core.

"Once we learned you were part shifter, Ananiel consulted Moira, Uriel's wife, the Seidr priestess."

"Moira." The name should have meant nothing to me. But suddenly it meant everything. The finest baker in the United States. Moira Connor of Sierra Madre, California, whose crumb cakes were legendary. I'd claimed to have ordered her cakes, but I couldn't recall why. Yet here was Sophia, confirming that I'd tasted Moira's offerings before and that Moira knew my lineage.

"She lives in Sierra Madre with the Connors," Sophia said. "She travels often, but she sent your gift, those caramel bites you devoured."

I flushed, remembering how I'd eaten three of them without thought. "They melted in my mouth."

"What's your favorite treat?" Sophia asked, motioning me to a bench under a wisteria-draped trellis.

I hesitated. Why did she care? "Caramel and white chocolate," I admitted.

She grinned. "Moira specializes in healing potions woven into her confections. She knows your anxiety and will replenish your supply of caramel chews before dawn."

I pressed my fingertips to my temples. "We're underwater, behind a domed barrier?"

Sophia's laugh was gentle. "Yes. But our docking station connects to pneumatic tubes that transfer us between Pantheons—Greek, Norse, Celestial, Sumerian, and more. You'll see."

I tried to steady my racing heart. Every fiber of my being screamed to flee, escape back to solid ground, to dry air, to freedom from this translucent prison. Hot tears of frustration threatened to break loose. I would not cry here.

"Come," Sophia said, touching my arm. "Let's move to the community center. I'll make you a cup of Gobi tea."

My mind crackled with tension. "Can you spike it?"

She laughed again, kindness shining in her eyes. "You'll never know if I do."

The community center was cozy, with rose-hued couches, beanbags scattered across a polished floor, a fireplace crackling amber light, and lace-curtained windows looking into the reef. I sank onto a couch, pressed my elbows to my knees, and fought to gather my thoughts.

Sophia handed me a steaming mug scented with lavender and herbs. I exhaled, willing my pulse to slow. Her voice was softer here.

"I remember my first visit," she confessed. "I thought I might drown, seeing nothing but endless water. Then I recalled the hidden habitats on Earth, the sea labs, research stations. I relaxed and embraced this world."

I clutched my silver locket, feeling its weight anchor me. Sophia's words were small ripples compared to the tsunami inside me. "My mother warned: protect the Cauldron of Wisdom. Hide your secret."

She placed a hand over mine, her touch warm. "Denying yourself may keep you safe short-term, but in time you will need the trust of those you seek to serve. Your destiny requires you to accept your true nature."

My throat tightened. I could not betray my mother's legacy, nor expose my wolf's vulnerability. Yet every moment here chipped at my resolve. My thoughts drifted to Ananiel—the electricity between us still crackled. My wolf hungered for a bond I had never known. I had missed my morning suppressant, and the moon was waxing toward its first quarter. The pull of the change, of the hunt, of the mating frenzy gnawed at me.

I needed to return to the surface before I shifted. If I transformed here—in these sacred halls—I would endanger everyone. My brothers had warned me: the Pack's tradition was ruthless. When the first frenzy came, males would fight for dominance. The chosen mate would claim her under the full moon, and no other would touch her. But until then, chaos reigned.

I set the mug down, determination hardening. "I must leave soon," I said, voice steady.

Sophia's gaze was sorrowful but understanding. "No one will force you to stay. But know this: hiding who you are will only delay your purpose. When the time is right, embrace your gift. The Silver Wolf was born for great things."

I bowed my head, tracing the triquetra. My breaths came in shallow bursts as I pictured the storm of transformation approaching. Ananiel's face, his stormy eyes, his steady warmth, flashed before me. If I remained, those eyes would call to my wolf, and I would slip beyond my control.

I rose, clutching the mug in both hands. The gentle steam curled around me like a promise. "Thank you, Sophia," I whispered.

She stood and offered her arm. "To the docking station?"

I nodded, steeling myself to step back into the crystalline city, into its secrets, its wonders, and its risks. My future lay somewhere between these walls of water and light, and the solid ground of home. Would I have the courage to accept both halves of myself before the moon demanded its due?

Chapter Eight

ANANIEL

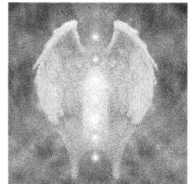

The full moon grew near, and Yahweh warned me to keep Grace away from the surface until after we started her transformation.

To be honest, doing anything my father requested caused my temper to rile. Based on what I'd learned of the custom of wolves, I had four days to wrap my mind around what needed to happen. I'd contact Seth of the Aiden wolf pack in Montana. I trusted him to help me select omega wolves who'd adhere to my command during the beginning phase of the waxing gibbous. I'd leave this afternoon and bring the men to Archipelago Island to get to know her.

I felt like a pimp selling Grace to the highest bidder. How could I address this with her? For it to work, she had to consent, Or I'd have no part in the transformation, no way would I participate in a nonconsensual agreement, no matter what was at stake. If needed, I'd find a way to force her shifter energy to release and I'd help her wolf complete the process, bringing the sacral light to the surface.

Unsure of how to proceed, I waited in my living quarters. Grace's anguish over her change caused my own nerves to grow tense. Tomorrow morning, Sophia would bring the caramel chews filled with soothing lavender root oil. They would ease Grace's panic attacks and allow her thoughts to focus without the debilitating anxiety.

Grace opened the door of her room, bringing me out of my musings. I faced her, and a flood of feeling filled me, roaring like the stormy seas. Being tied to her through the sigil spell signature, I experienced her insecurities about what was to happen in the next few days. Did she feel my own excited emotions? Closing my eyes, I inhaled the scent of her freshly bathed body and fought the desire stirring my hardened cock. Possessive awareness, like rooted vines, tightened at the thought of others taking their pleasure with her. I dreaded this conversation, but the sooner we understood each other and established the ground rules than the sooner I could leave for Montana with a clear conscience.

Grace's jade green eyes sparkled with fire, her chin angled up, and she met my gaze with a determination that amused me. To my surprise, she controlled her anxiety and kept her emotions in check. In fact, I felt none of her earlier vulnerability. She'd switched personas and came across every bit the powerful woman she was. This wasn't the same frightened female I'd spoken with this morning.

Grace entered my sitting room and sat in the armchair where I sometimes counseled the nephilim during their months at the guild.

"Ananiel, Sophia took me on a tour of the docking station. You can send me home." She picked up a magazine of druid spells.

I took the other armchair, which created a sense of formality between us. "If anyone sees you, then the mages will know of your rescue. For now, they believe you are in a comatose state."

Grace's fingers twitched slightly, and her heart beat faster.

Her feelings swarmed through me like a school of piranhas. Adrenaline filled her system, and I felt her urge to run and bolt. Her eyes grew round with fright, like a caged animal. I sensed her wolf calling to me, but I wasn't sure how to help her.

"As President of the United States, I'm warning you that holding me against my will is an international offense. You willingly risk the lives of the Nephilim because you don't want me to return to the capital city."

"Ms. Isaeva, if you return—you not only risk the guardians—you endanger your own people. If that happens, the shifters and magicals stand little chance of blending into human society."

"What do you know of our dilemma?" Her expression showed suspicion.

"The warlock who stuffed you in the trunk of your car will steal your supernatural power. If that occurs, few will survive the destructive enslavement that will plunge every pantheon of this galaxy. My words hit her hard, and I felt the chink in her armor slip as awareness dawned in her eyes.

"You know what I am?" Grace's chin angled up, and she met my gaze. "Then you know I am in danger of shifting at any moment. I take suppressants like birth control to prevent the desire to mate."

"We need to discuss the frenzy and what that means."

Her face blanched as her gaze fixed on me.

"Hmm...I don't want to discuss this matter with you."

A mischievous smile curved around the corners of my mouth, and I imagined her luscious body wet and writhing for my touch. I had to take control of my emotions and show her I was there to support her, no matter how she stirred my desire.

"Within the hour, I'm meeting with the Aiden wolf pack to ensure your transition is safe."

The toe of her sandal tapped a frustrated rhythm on the floor. "Pardon me?"

Grace crossed her arms over her chest and glanced out the window and back to me. "You're an arrogant jerk. I have no intention of succumbing to my wolf's needs. Go to the surface and bring me the bottle of pills on my bedside."

"Not happening. Your wolf needs to come to the surface. She has a job to do, and you, my love, have obligations to fulfill."

"And what does that mean?"

"After the transformation, you'll assume leadership of the shifters." A wave of panic washed over her, and fear lurked in the depths of her eyes. I placed my elbows on my knees, waiting for a breath. "The entire supernatural and human realms depend on you for their survival. So, my alpha wolf, you have little choice but to submit to the transformation and face your destiny."

She glared. "Why the Aiden pack?" Her head twisted around, her eyes widened, sparkling with shock and something else.

Her reaction intrigued me. "I do business with the alpha, and I trust him."

"My brothers live in Park City, Montana. One's a wildlife researcher and veterinarian, and occasionally he works with the three Yellowstone packs. Ask Roger for more pills."

I rose from the armchair and offered my hand to Grace. "I'm in charge of seeing you through this ordeal."

"I want to go with you to Yellowstone." She stood to face me without flinching.

"You'll be recognized." I grinned with a distinctly male satisfaction that she'd already succumbed in her heart, if not her mind.

"If we stay within the wolf community, I'll be safe."

"No." A note of triumph rang in my voice.

She glared at me with a furious desire to rip out my throat. "You're an ass." She snarled, refusing to take my hand.

I'd pushed Grace into doing what she needed to do. What worried me now was my role. If I didn't deal with my rage and allow her to warm my bitter heart, we would fail. The Kundalini dragon would fall prey to Diablo and the dark forces.

"While I go to Yellowstone, have dinner with the guardians. Get to know their strengths, and learn who they are? This group of Nephilim practices the art of politics. They will return with you to the White House, and you will appoint them to key positions throughout your administration."

A frown wrinkled between her brows. "And when did you become in charge of appointees to the US government?"

"The moment I saved your lovely arse and brought you here."

"I'd like to train with the women in the morning. Plan to provide me with a knife and workout gear. Tonight, I'll sleep in Sophia and Ariel's room since they've left for the day."

I conceded for now. "Upon my return, I'll place them in your room, but in the future, you will sleep here with me."

"I doubt it."

She walked out, letting the door slam behind her.

Chapter Nine

GRACE

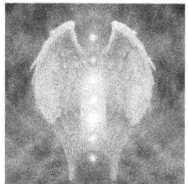

Throughout the night, I'd tossed and turned, never getting comfortable. Every time I fell asleep, images of my body being stuffed into the trunk reminded me of the trouble I faced. I needed to get back to the White House. Ananiel said little, and I surmised at least two mages had access to classified information. I wasn't sure if my double was supernatural or just a hired replacement to be disposed of when she was no longer needed.

I clutched the coverlet close to my chest.

What really had me worried was my transformation. The first adult shift of my wolf. I really wanted to talk to my brothers and find out the mystery behind the traditional pack ceremony. As a rogue wolf, I'd always stayed alone, refusing to shift and take part with the other females in their selection of mates. I had lived among the humans since I was a child. Having been raised Russian Orthodox, I was ashamed at the idea of indulging in such animalistic pleasures of multiple partners.

I needed to ask Roger what would happen if I refused and shifted alone. I wanted to mate for love. And the few lovers I'd taken over the years left me empty. Never would I abandon myself to the frenzy I'd heard other shifter women describe during their first change. I never lost control and had no intention of letting my libido dictate my behavior.

I stepped out of bed, washed my face, and donned the workout clothes Ananiel left me. A ribbon of warmth edged its way around my heart at his thoughtful gesture. A V-42 stiletto fighting knife. I couldn't imagine how he'd gotten his hands on such a beautiful replica. I wanted to wrap my fingers around the stacked leather handle and feel the power of the blade soar through my body. The unique chrome vanadium sliced through steak like soft butter. On the leather sheath, he'd imprinted a silver wolf with my name. Instead of a metal clasp, a string of leathered rawhide enabled me to tie the sheath around my thigh.

There was a tap on the door.

"Yes?"

The lyrical lilt of Sophia's voice charmed me. I hoped we'd become friends. I'd need her to lock me in if the heat of pain became intolerable. "Come in."

She handed me a bag of caramel chews that Ananiel had Moira make for me to use instead of the Zoloft. "Moira, with her magical touch, comes to our rescue. Her message said that she and Uriel will attend the special party welcoming you to the family."

"Family?" I asked, not sure how to respond.

"Ananiel is one of the five Sarim princes."

"Four brothers." I couldn't wrap my mind around the events of the last twenty-four hours.

Jeffrey poked his head in the door. "Madam President, breakfast is served in the solarium."

"Join me." I turned to Sophia, not wanting to be alone.

"Hot cup of tea and one of Moira's croissants sounds heavenly."

She looped her arm into mine, showing me the way to the indoor garden.

Artificial lamps lit the room enclosed with stained glass. The lush foliage climbed the sides of the wall. On one side, the garden featured various herbs and vegetables. Beautiful peperomias and peace lilies filled another area. Two covered plates sat on a table surrounded by sword ferns. My lungs tightened, positive I'd not get enough air as a wall of water reminded me of my need to escape.

"Sophia, could you show me how to program one chute? I really must return to D.C. and get back to work."

"Why don't you train with the ladies this morning, walk around, and get to know the guild? Inside the classroom, Ariel's giving a lesson on American politics. I'm sure he could use your help. It'll give you the opportunity to study the male guardians and check out the cadets who will be your new security force."

"So, I take it that means no." I pursed my lips in a slight pucker, hoping she'd feel sorry for me.

Sophia leaned closer and offered a blueberry bite. "I know you're frustrated, but if we return too soon, we risk failure. More is at stake than the presidential office."

"What aren't you telling me?"

"I'll leave that to Ananiel. When you're comfortable, Ariel could use your help with preparing your new security staff." Sophia paused and put a hand on her hip. "During your workout, select two women who will be your security inside the presidential suites."

Resigned I wasn't finding a way back to the surface yet, I might as well hone my fighting skills. We finished our breakfast, and I followed her to the fitness arena. Teams parried in twos, threes, and fours.

The tallest woman turned and pulled the blade from the wall.

"Hi Sophia."

"Juna, this is Grace, the President of the United States."

Our gazes met, held, and I had the strangest sense of déjà vu. Every cell in my body went on red alert. These women weren't fucking around. I sized up her lean, muscular body, her calm demeanor, and the glint in her eye. She wasn't human. Her scent held a powerful hint of salt, much like the briny smell I sensed around Ananiel.

"I'll be your trainer."

"You're in expert hands," Sophia said, leaving out the rear door. "I'll be in the guild classroom after your workout. Come find me."

I stretched my legs and then did a series of squats, warming up my quads.

"Any good with knives?" Juna asked as she circled the mat.

The woman sized me up like I'd checked her. No doubt Juna could block or barricade any surprise blows I might send her way, so I needed the element of surprise. I waited for her to make the first strike. She eased up on my left, and I sensed she was attempting to obstruct my view of the other fighters.

To prevent exposure, I flipped my body mid-air and pulled my blade from its sheath to face off with a dark-haired beauty who planned on taking me from behind.

"Stand down," I called to Juna, who stood to the side of me. "My blade kisses her throat. One slip—and my dagger will slice like butter through her pretty mocha neck."

In one swift movement, my blade dropped from my hand, and Juna's blade touched the base of my back, where in an instant she could sever my spinal cord. Damn, this girl was good.

My wolf growled, fighting to be released from her confinement. My skin tingled, and my claws extended. If the transition happened unexpectedly, I wasn't sure if I could control my nature.

I was a predator, and if prey ran from me, my instinct would be to attack. My canines sharpened, drawing blood from my tongue. I closed my eyes and tapped the fighter's forearm, telling her I'd submit.

Juna handed me a towel. "You okay?"

"I'm fine." I snatched the towel from her hand. Losing was something I hated. "Impressive, I thought I had you beat when my blade was against her throat."

"I'm Kai. You'll have to teach me how to do that kick-ass flip." Kai took the other towel Juna offered.

"You've got it."

Kai left and rejoined the others in their routines.

"I'd like you on my security team."

"Thought you might." Juna opened the fridge and tossed me a bottle of water. "I'm here at nine every morning. I sensed your wolf-predator nature. She'll need to get to know me if we're going to be on the same team."

I froze and faced her. "You know I'm a shifter?"

"Everyone here knows. You're on an island of Nephilim hybrid water angels."

Juna joined the other women, leaving me to stare dumbfounded at her revelation. I sensed the beginnings of the transformation, and a blind panic gnawed at me. My heart raced as I suspended my breath. I didn't want to lose control to the wolf and cause harm to innocent people.

Chapter Ten

GRACE

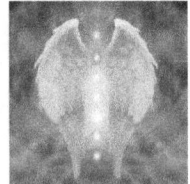

Standing at the docking station, I still hadn't recovered from my near shift this morning. What if I hurt someone? I had to discuss this with Ananiel, but I didn't know how he'd take it. Probably lock me up in my room until I finally transitioned.

A series of lights and a horn blasted. Ananiel arrived with my two brothers and three other men I didn't recognize. I knew they were wolf shifters and meant to help with my transition.

Holy shit, I had no idea what was happening. Mages were after my light. My hormones were freaking out, and if someone didn't intervene, I'd seduce every unrelated male in my vicinity.

And, if I was honest, the hot Sarim prince made my wolf howl with a desire to claim him as my very own. What in the hell would I do? I wanted to go home, turn back the clock, and deny any of this reality.

Roger, caught my eye and our gazes held, calming my stressed-out wolf. Compassion reflected in his golden-brown eyes. Dustin, was my favorite. He'd always understood my fears after our parents' deaths. Roger, the oldest, took on the responsibility of caring for us. Deep down, I think he felt guilty for leaving me with our father's family. They'd never really liked my parents' lifestyle.

Once my parents were gone, Cheryl Cameron, my father's sister, denied my supernatural existence and groomed me to follow the family into politics.

Now that I was president, I had to open the public's rose-colored glasses to the needs of all species. If legislation passed denying them their birth-right as U.S. citizens then we'd never progress as a nation. I feared isolated pockets would begin warring with each other for dominance.

As more magical mingled with humans, the tension between the groups rose. And for the supernaturals, hunters plagued our communities, killing us for sport. Fear of outright war loomed on the horizon if the paranormal council didn't find a way to appease everyone with a stake in the outcome.

On top of all this, I had to face a fucking warlock who was determined to use me like a siphon hose and suck the energy from my soul.

I embraced my brothers and allowed them to soothe the wolf inside. She recognized family.

Ananiel waited at a distance with the other three men.

I appreciated the moment.

Roger held out a bottle of suppressants. "I made you another batch."

I sighed in relief. I didn't know if it was too late to prevent the shift, but I'd try.

"How are you, little sister?"

"I've had better days."

"Will these stop the transition from happening?"

With a heavy sigh, he stood back, still holding my hands.

"Not completely, but it will help with the sexual cravings."

"Why not?" I stammered.

"The waxing moon started two days ago, and it's too late to prevent the change. If you deny the frenzy, you're gonna be in a lot of pain."

"I fear the wolf's power. This morning, my fangs and claws protruded. First, just a tingling in my fingers. Then, the hair on my arms turned a pure silver."

"Your eyes have changed. They've become brighter, more like a field of shamrocks." Roger smiled and cupped my chin in his hand. "I've missed you."

Dustin moved Roger aside and placed his large hands around my cheeks. He kissed my forehead. "I see our mother in you, her spirit. It's time to honor who you are and embrace your wolf."

"I can't."

"The legends foretold of a powerful silver wolf who will bring a new world into being." Pride gleamed in Roger's eyes.

"I'm not the shifter leader." I pulled from my two brothers and glanced in Ananiel's direction.

"Ananiel believes you are his archeia. Together, the two of you have a role to play." Roger squeezed my arm.

Dustin took my hand. "Trust in him, allow him into your heart, and become who you are."

"What if he doesn't want me?" I clenched my fist and felt the jaw tighten.

"He also fears your rejection, but the prophecy predicts the angel and the wolf will change the future."

"Then why the sexual frenzy, if destiny has chosen for me?" My voice dripped with sarcastic disappointment that I still had to go through this ritual of lust. I didn't enjoy submitting to any preordained concept. I could change everything, and I refused to cower to the gods.

"Destiny goes only so far; you still must desire Ananiel with a pure love."

"That settles the problem; I refuse to fall in love with anyone. Look what happened to our parents."

"Ananiel isn't our father; he won't ask you to deny who you are." Roger rubbed the muscles in the back of his neck.

"How? I can't accomplish this change if the American people feel I've lied to them. The country will oust me as president.

"Trust in the gifts of the triquetra." Dustin lifted the locket and traced the intricate Viking design. "Mom gave you the necklace at birth, believing one day you'd grow to understand its curse."

"Brother, you speak in riddles. Mom warned me to keep my wolf secret."

"After you finish the transition, you will understand clearly when you mark your intended mate."

"I take it, you have no plans of helping me return home." I whispered so Ananiel wouldn't overhear.

"My hard-headed sister, you are right where you're supposed to be. Fate is preparing you to take your role as the shifter leader of the supernatural community."

Chest out, shoulders back. Roger made direct eye contact, ensuring I understood every word. Jaw clamped tight, I gave him a pure look of menace.

"The Aiden pack has agreed to protect you with their lives and accept you into their pack as an equal alpha female."

A pleased glint reached Dustin's eyes.

"Meaning I'm to choose within the pack if I refuse to accept Ananiel."

"As an alpha female, you select whom you mate with, but you must decide. I'm positive one of Aiden's wolves will satisfy you if Ananiel displeases you."

Roger smiled as if he already understood my genuine desires.

I growled in protest. Determined to make my own decisions.

"Ananiel's not a wolf."

"When he saved your life, he bargained and accepted a part of your soul. The spell-caster bound him with a piece of your wolf sigil signature. Neither of you will be satisfied without the other."

He'd punched the wind out of my sails. My argument disappeared.

"No other will touch you without your consent," Dustin said in a tone meant to reassure me.

Roger spoke with the same self-assured attitude as any alpha wolf. He motioned to Ananiel; they were ready for the others to join their discussion.

When the wolf shifters joined us, I grew silent. Ananiel reached for my arm. "I promise nothing will harm you, but you're not returning to the surface until your wolf appears and begins the shift."

"Let go of me." I thrust out of his grip and reached for my knife with a predator's need to dominate.

"Calm down." My brothers sidled to either side of me to protect me should any of the alpha shifters show dominance.

Blood coursed through my veins and I wanted to lower my canines into their necks, showing them who was in charge.

Ananiel rushed toward me, grasped my hand, and flashed.

A spiraling effect raced through me before my vision cleared and I was standing in his sitting room.

"I've placed a guard at the doors. Why don't you get some rest? I'll be back before the evening meal, and we'll talk, if you're ready to see logic."

With that, he flashed out of the room, leaving me speechless and steaming with fury.

Chapter Eleven

GRACE

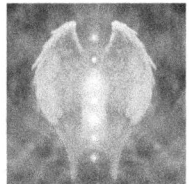

I paced the floor and couldn't believe he'd left me in here for over two hours like he intended to teach me a lesson. He'd learn I wasn't so easily tamed.

A dim blue light appeared, and Ananiel came through the door with a trident in his hand.

Wisps of his dark hair rose off his shoulder. Power filled the room, and I felt small in his presence.

I took in his attire. The pleated skirt of bronze barely covered his male anatomy. Those full legs made my mouth water in anticipation of running my tongue along his inner thighs. Liquid heat charged right to my core and any anger I still harbored disappeared in his magnificent beauty.

"Tomorrow evening, my brothers and Moira will be here for dinner. Ariel and Sophia will join us as well as your brothers and the omega wolves."

His compelling smoky eyes, the firm features, the confident set of his shoulders make me melt.

He took me in his arms.

"What happened to set you off this morning?"

A strange apprehension crawled up my spine, and the ache of not being with Ananiel pained me. I swallowed the thick lump lodged in my throat. "My wolf started to shift."

"Did you lose control?" His face softened with real concern.

"Juna, I, and Kai challenged each other to a fight. When Juna disarmed me, a silver streak of energy surged through my body, and I felt the predator rise. I feared if either woman ran, my wolf would treat them like prey." Threads of silver glimmer still shimmered in my fingertips and I trembled. I gazed up at him shaking uncontrollably. "What if I'd caused one of your nephilim harm?"

"Your wolf will soon learn the difference; she reacted to your intense emotions. Trust me."

His tongue traced the soft fullness of my lips. Teasing, pushing me to open my mouth. A need stabbed so urgently in my core. My wolf—she wanted to play. My lips parted and his mouth covered mine hungrily, his kiss sending spirals of ecstasy through me, making my body ache. He kissed the pulsing hollow at the base of my throat and my canines dropped grazing his shoulder. *What the hell?* I had to pull myself together and stop this insanity before I claimed him.

A knock at the door startled me out of my recklessness as I eased from the room to put a fair amount of distance between us.

"I asked Jeffrey to bring a few of your clothes and toiletries."

His consideration of my needs warmed my heart and I wanted to believe he could keep me safe.

Jeffrey entered the room with my make-up bag and a suitcase. "If you need other items, give me a list, and I'll bring them to you.

He set the suitcase by the door.

"Thanks, Jeffrey."

"At your service, Madame President." He backed out the door and left them to continue where they'd left all before his arrival.

"I appreciate your kindness, but I don't plan on being here for long."

His forehead furrowed and worry lines showed in the tightness of his muscles.

"You're not going anywhere but right into my arms."

His smoldering gaze sent scorching heat, and I understood his intention.

"You're not leaving this room anytime soon."

My wolf howled with pleasure, and a sharp ache filled my core. A sexual desire so strong hit. If Ananiel didn't take me right now, I thought my body would burst with agonizing pain.

Ananiel's erection pushed hard against me, demanding attention in the same way I did. His need was as strong as my own. Our tongues danced as each of our bodies melted against the other. Demanding.

A guttural moan escaped Ananiel.

The sound made me growl as my desire heightened.

His strong fingers clasped my neck, pulling me closer. His mouth crushed against mine drinking his fill. The kiss sent my hormones raging. I wanted this stormy man to rip off my clothes and ram his hard cock inside. "Take these off, now," I growled.

He pulled back and murmured, "Slow down, wolf girl, you'll get everything you need before the night is over."

I couldn't, and I forced my tongue inside his mouth. Teasing him, I sucked its hot length, enjoying the feel of him. I wanted his cock inside my mouth. I wanted to taste him, swallow him, and make him surrender to me. "I need you now."

Ananiel grasped my arms and disengaged himself.

The strained look in his gaze warned me he didn't like being out of control. I smiled inwardly because right now I wanted to claim him as my own, make him submit to me even though I'd just pronounced to my brothers I had no intention of choosing yet.

I couldn't explain the magnetism that drew me to him as my fingers reached under his fustanella and filled my hands with his large balls. I grasped his cock. "Take me in your angel form."

His beautiful bronze wings emerged, and nothing could prepare me for the wrath and fury of his body. He sealed his lips over mine, taking possession of my mouth.

Deep inside my mind, I knew what we shared was not love, it was madness. I was disturbed by the raw power surging through me. Blood throbbed in my veins with a scarlet web of desire that I doubted would ever be satisfied.

"My wolf," I mumbled.

Ananiel removed my hand from his cock and readjusted his clothing. Frantic, mindless I was helpless to resist him as he slid his fingers in my leggings and felt for my wetness.

"Oh, yes. More."

"Not yet."

His wet fingers grazed my cheek in such tenderness that the beast inside settled down at his touch.

Taking both my wrists, he held them above my head. "Do not move your hands until I tell you to, or I'll leave you tonight to suffer through the agony alone. Do you understand?"

I nodded. I'd become a slave to my biological need.

He unbuttoned each button, taking his time as his mouth kissed my neck.

Unable to take the slow temptation of his tongue, I started to lower my hands. He stopped. "Leave your hands above your head until I tell you to put them down."

His sultry voice made me want to come, but he'd demanded I wait. I eagerly obeyed him. My wolf relished in his torment. Ananiel pushed me to the brink, then pulled back. His finger slid down my belly as his teeth nibbled my breast making me squirm. I wanted to grab him and tell him to get down on his knees and lick my damn pussy.

"My, my we're a bossy one."

Had he just read my thoughts? "You said you couldn't read minds, so how did you know what I wanted?"

"Your arousal, so sweet and eager, desires release. I feel your want, your need, and your passion."

His finger hooked into my leggings and removed them from my body.

I stood there in lacy, red panties, dripping wet and in need. "I want to touch you. Please," I begged, needing to feel his flesh under my hands.

"Not just yet." His hot breath lingered over my pussy.

I looked up to realize the omega wolves stood in the doorway with their cocks in hand. I wanted to tell them to go away, but I was hungry for the forbidden. I wanted these men to touch me with Ananiel.

"You enjoy them watching?"

"Yes."

"Tell the wolf shifters what you want."

"I want all three to touch me at the same time." My lust was an emotional hunger that could not be denied.

"Like this?" He slid his fingers inside me.

I writhed against his hand, thrusting my hips, wanting so much more.

"No cock will fuck you; but mine. Do you understand, my archeia?" as he snapped my panties off.

My wolf howled in agony as the sexual drive coursed through me. The frenzy was upon me. Fire burned in my loins, and I couldn't stop the ache forming between my legs. My swollen clit throbbed with a pulsating pain that cried to be licked. "Please, Ananiel. Allow no other; keep me for yourself. I choose you, but I need..." The ache between my thighs grew more and more insistent.

"Embrace me." Our gazes met.

He lowered me to the bed. Ananiel spread my thighs wide as the three men gazed down at the pink folds of my pussy."

"Kiss her," Ananiel told the golden-haired warrior.

The first omega's tongue circled my drenched bud and I gasped.

"Come, my sweet, it's only the beginning. Now, you will come and come and come until every nerve-ending screams for my cock to take you."

He sheathed his tongue into me and I arched into the golden haired omega. My body spun into frenzy as he licked and sucked, pleasure shot through me as I gave in to the moment. A convulsive wave gripped me, and I screamed, "Ananiel."

"We're only getting started."

Ananiel stood back and our eyes gazed into each other's.

His power of light surrounded him in a picture of spectral beauty.

"Do you enjoy what he's doing?"

The one with the night owl tattoo stroked me with his fingers while the other took my nipples between his tongue and teeth, hardening them.

Ananiel eyes glowed with lust.

I gasped with each measured thrust of the omega's finger. My toes curled, and my back arched as I came again. Both men thrust their fingers into me, bringing me to the greatest climax I'd ever had. I went spiraling as my body only craved more.

"On your knees." Ananiel demanded. "Tell me how much you liked it."

I obeyed and he stood behind me and gripped my hips in his large hands. Shame ramrodded its nasty tendrils into my thoughts at having to admit to the pleasure surging through me. My aunt's words rang in my mind, telling me how dirty shifters were and how wrong the ceremony was. I was a whore for submitting to the transformation. Agony filled me and clenched my stomach.

"Answer me."

The three male omegas stood in front of me with extended cocks. "Yes. I want more."

"I will punish you for wanting more. You're a bad girl for wanting this transition. You're a whore."

How did he know the dark images that tortured me since childhood? "Punish me. I shouldn't enjoy this. The frenzy is wrong. Punish me."

Ananiel slapped my ass.

My cheeks burned under his hand.

"Did you like them touching you?"

I bit down on my lip, fighting the need for more. What was wrong with me?

He slapped the other cheek.

My breath hissed, a sound that was half-pain, half-pleasure. Even more powerful sensations built and throbbed. The tension inside me ready to explode. "I'm not bad."

"You're beautiful, Grace, and your wolf waits for you to embrace her. Stop punishing yourself. You're my archeia, Accept what you are doing is right." His hand once again slapped my ass.

The pain, mixed with pleasure, made my heart pound, and my body quiver. When he slapped my ass again, I saw stars. My cheeks on fire until his hot tongue licked the burning sensation away. Every nerve-ending quivered, and an orgasm hit full force.

"That's it, my love."

"More." I cried.

"Kiss the middle one's cock."

My mouth went around his shaft, and I ran my tongue along the mushroom head.

"Good girl."

Ananiel moved from behind me and I straddled the omega with the night owl tattooed on his chest. His mouth covered my clit.

Ananiel stood to the side of the bed and ran his fingers over my ass.

"I want you to," I cried.

"Like this?" And he poured a cool gel along the crack in my ass. He spoke to the last omega. "Come stand on the other side of her and insert your fingers into her wet passage. The first omega fucked my mouth, the other sucked, and I couldn't believe the glorious sensation rushing through my body as the third entered his fingers inside me.

Ananiel's rubbed my lower back, his hand slid lower, and his thumb penetrated my opening. I thrust my behind at him, daring him to take me deeper and harder.

My wolf wanted this as Ananiel pushed inside. The pleasure against the thin lining was like riding on the edge of a cliff about to fall off. While I enjoyed the sensation of Ananiel's penetration into my ass, I relaxed into a delicious submission as the omega's fingers pushed to the same rhythm that Ananiel set. I swallowed the omega's cock enjoying his thrust inside my throat. He came and I swallowed. Then the night owl shifter moved from underneath me and put his cock in my mouth.

He moaned in release.

The third omega removed his fingers, leaving an aching need I still wanted filled. "Take the third cock. Suck him hard."

"Take her hair and fuck her hard in the mouth." Ananiel demanded.

He slapped my cheek.

I pushed against him and took more of the man's cock into my mouth. The other two spread the folds of my pussy, finding me slippery. One pinched my throbbing nub and worked it, then both men inserted two strong fingers. In and out as Ananiel continued to love my ass. They plunged inside me, igniting my body in a way I'd never experienced. An explosion of come filled my mouth tasting like peppery spice.

His hands went to my dangling breast.

Ananiel leaned over my back and bit my shoulder.

Erotic oblivion gripped me, sending me over the edge as my body writhed in orgasmic overload.

I panted with each measured thrust until I came nonstop and gasped for air. Suddenly, I collapsed onto the bed and growled.

Each male moved away.

My claws extended.

My body twitched.

As my limbs changed into paws, I twisted in agony.

My snout extended, and suddenly my ears pointed. I screamed.

The wolf shifters smiled and left me alone with Ananiel.

As a wolf, I scramble onto all fours, shook, and jumped from the bed. Ananiel stood close to the bedroom door, I moved toward him determined to claim my mate.

His burnt crimson wings flamed from his back, and he disappeared from my room.

Chapter Twelve

ANANIEL

Unaware of what to expect, I sucked in a breath; the silver wolf with shamrock eyes filled me with awe and dread. Was I ready to take this creature on and become her mate? Leaving her alone after her ordeal, I took a moment to compose my own turbulent feelings. The frenzy of the transformation sated, she'd soon attempt to claim me. The smell of her arousal was like a drug, and I could not deny the pull of my archeia. I was denied her touch and love, and for a thousand years, my heart ached with that emptiness.

I moved around my bed and sat on the edge of the mattress. I left the door open in case she needed me. My wings receded into my back, and my armor changed into a black t-shirt and Wranglers.

The atmosphere grew dense, and I sensed Grace's wolf in the room. I quirked the right side of my mouth in a knowing grin.

Grace placed her paws on my chest, and her rough tongue licked my face. Then, she shifted back. Her hair now had several silver streaks mixed with her shiny black hair.

She leaned in and kissed me. Her sweet mouth worked her magic on me. Our savage tongues circled like two predators staking their territory. To entice her wolf spirit, I flashed to a small estuary hidden on the far side of the island.

Predators loved challenges, and I couldn't wait to see how long she'd take to pickup my scent. A fabulous opportunity to test her heightened tracking skills. I leaned against a stump and allowed myself to rest. A nap would revitalize my tired body.

The rustle of leaves alerted me Grace was in the mangrove trees. Her sense of smell was strong as she maneuvered through the salty stilt roots that branched and looped around the trunks of the trees. I watched as her snout rose into the air.

She climbed over the aerial roots that hovered creating a perfect hiding spot.

My loins stirred with excitement. My beautiful Grace's silver fur sparkled like glistening diamonds. The strength of her wolf radiated around her. Her joy reached deep into my own heart.

I watched in fascination as she shifted. Her luscious body glimmered even brighter, the transformation making her human form grander, stronger than before. Her long hair hung over her breasts like a beautiful siren. I knew I was lost in lustful desire.

"Sneaky of you to make me find you. I'll have to punish you for your deviousness."

Her sultry voice dripped with desire, making my cock stand at attention.

"You're late. I expected you five minutes ago." I walked to her, weaving my fingers through her hair and bringing my mouth over hers. "If anyone's going to punish, it will be me." I slapped her sweet round ass, the roar of the crashing waves outside the dome filling my soul.

Our bodies connected like fresh and salt water, both needing each other to thrive. Our mouths were alive with wet heat. Arousal pressed against my jeans as she slid one slender leg over my thigh and rubbed her wet pussy all over me. As she unbuckled my jeans, releasing my shaft. I breathed deeply as her fingers closed over my hard flesh, making my swollen organ burn with desire.

I fought the urge to climax and watch me come all over her rose-colored nipples. Nipples I wanted to feast on. Her hand continued to move in a steady rhythm, driving me wild. I gritted my teeth against the oncoming sensation, a rising crescendo. I clasped her hips and growled as I came in a rush. She'd taken the power, turning this game against me and forcing me to surrender.

"I told you I'd punish you." She smiled.

I felt her inner pleasure in making me lose control.

I pulled off my shirt and wiped my seed off her sexy flesh. For the moment, she could bask in her satisfaction. Before the night ended, she'd be screaming my name and begging me to allow her to orgasm.

"I'll be right back." I flashed to her room, picked up the clothes she'd left on the floor, and flashed back to the estuary. If our love proved real and we survived the week until the full moon. I wanted her to know how to protect herself against a witch's spell. Now that she'd shifted, the mages would sense her change and realize she'd escaped. I needed to talk with Moira and have her make a protection charm for Grace.

"Thanks." She pulled on the pair of black leggings and a tunic. "Where are we?"

"Poseidon's Cove. It's the portal to the Olympian realm."

She gave me a sexy, wicked smile, both invitation and challenge. I relished the change in her features and reached my hand around those streaks of silver that blended in her black hair.

She tugged on her lower lip. "My hair doesn't make me look too old, does it?"

"The frosted streaks enhance your high cheekbones."

She cocked her head, squinting. "You're different."

I gave her an easy nod, breaking the mental trance between us. For the first time in a long while, I wanted to explore possibilities with her. My goal was to protect her from the surface. I wanted her, and the thought consumed me. I wanted to tell the world to vanish, so we could have some peace. But that wouldn't happen. Within a few days, she'd return to the White House, where the real challenge waited. "During your transition, I experienced the pain and joy of your emotions. I experienced every frenzy moment until you reached the pinnacle of release."

A flush of red colored her cheeks. "The frenzy was quite a ride, but I couldn't have completed the shift if not for you."

I took pleasure in her words, because sharing her like that was never, ever, happening again if I had any choice in the decision. She was mine. "Have you developed any new skills?"

She turned toward the water. "I'm not afraid."

The tide was rising. In an hour, the rising tide would hide this area. I took her hand and intertwined our fingers.

Chapter Thirteen

ANANIEL

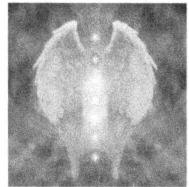

My radio pinged.

"Your guests arrived in chute twelve and chute three," Gavin said.

I suspected our enemies might send spies through the portal docking station, so I placed extra cadets on chute three. Early today, Zadkiel informed me that the mages learned of Grace's rescue. Trepidation filled my thoughts, and I clenched my fist, unsure of how to protect her.

My ten brothers came through the chute like a herd of wild bulls. You'd think none of them had any manners. Zadkiel led the princes. Each angel sported a navy-blue, diamond-tip American flag bow tie. I'm sure in honor of Grace.

After disembarking from the docks, they surrounded me with clapping hands and high fives.

"It's about time this motley crew got here." A festive energy surrounded the angels, and I knew each of my brothers sought to meet their one true spirit-mate.

"We're eager to meet the second archeia. If you haven't screwed it up with your stormy moods."

I gave Luc a look that said he could go right back to hell if he didn't keep his sarcasm to himself. I couldn't remember in the last millennium when all my brothers had been on the island at one time.

The horn blared. Whirlpool six signaled an arrival from the Nordic pantheon.

"Unexpected visitor. Should I block their entrance into the docking station?" Gavin asked.

"Keep the shield in place until I get a look."

"I'll be right back." I moved down the pathway to chute six.

To my surprise, the Wyrd sisters of the Nordic pantheon, accompanied by their shape-shifting wolf companions, strode through and stepped onto the landing.

Urd, the giant goddess of the past, held an intricate tapestry revealing a rainbow image of the kundalini dragon. In the base, an image of the red jasper gem weaved into the dragon's spinal core. Four cavities lay empty, waiting for the gems of each of the Sarim princes and their archeia.

I faltered under the power of the magical wards surrounding the Norns. Verdandi drew three runess over the magnetic shield, and the force field faded. The tapestry dematerialized.

Zadkiel and I greeted the Norns while our brothers flashed to the dining hall. "Welcome, Urd, Verdandi, and Skuld. Your presence honors the Sarim princes." I bowed in reverence to the high priestesses of the Nordic pantheon.

"We come with a warning and blessing for the silver wolf."

I clenched my hands, wary of the dangers facing Grace. "Join us for dinner."

Zadkiel took the older crone's hand and walked her off the platform. "Will you be accompanying Grace during her wolf transformation?"

"No." The witches turned to me and cackled. "The Storm Watcher has ridden that tsunami wave without our help."

Skuld gave a wink.

The light blinked. Uriel and Moira came through chute one.

Moira wore an elegant winter-green gown that matched her beautiful golden-red hair.

She bowed a respectful curtsy. "The fate of the Norns—what brings you to Archipelago Island?"

"Seidr priestess, I bring hard news to bear. News that will cause you great distress," Skuld said, gliding so beautifully in her white pearl gown. "We request council with you and Ananiel."

Urd and Verdandi, fates of the past and the present, watched as the three wolves shifted into attractive males varying in age. "Would you be so kind as to find clothes for our men?"

I reached for my communicator. "Jeffery, we have an unexpected guest. Arrange another table of six."

"Gavin, will you see to everyone's comfort while Moira and I speak with the witches?"

In a moment, the docking station emptied.

"The three Norn wolves are her ancestors and will stay here on Archipelago Island and then return to the White House with Grace," Verdandi stated. "They'll work as spies and protectors until the kundalini rises for the second time. We cannot risk Grace and the imprisonment of her soul."

"Sarim prince of the celestial heavens, your courage in saving her life and accepting the sigil signature magic into your own soul reveals an integrity of heart." Skuld, the woman who foretold the future, smiled at me.

Her words wound like silken threads around my heart. They softened the edges of my soul. I hadn't felt honored in years, and even the surprise appearance of Yahweh couldn't dampen my pleasure at seeing so many people come to meet my archeia. I'd planned a family meal with my brothers and the Nephilim cadets. Apparently, our simple dinner is growing into a ballroom affair with tuxedos and gowns.

Skuld moved closer to Moira and me. "A word in private before we enter the festivities."

Uriel kissed Moira and whispered in her ear. Since their mating, he'd become quite possessive of his bride.

Moira tucked her hand around my biceps and leaned in. "Powerful magic is at play for the Nordic Norns to leave the world tree."

"The appearance of the covens, I assume."

Skuld and her two sisters took my other arm, and the other five of us flashed to my quarters for privacy. I tapped on Grace's door to make sure we were alone. When no answer came, I peered inside. No doubt she was with Sophia getting dressed. Worry snaked through me at the danger ahead.

Skuld's slender fingers moved with lightning precision, drawing an intricate weave with strings of blue and purple threads whirling into knots. Ruby red, the color of blood, oozed in sporadic splotches.

Moira drew a variety of sigils and Nordic runic images.

To my surprise, their faces carried an urgency that disturbed me so I couldn't explain. I shuddered as their protective magical wards weaved throughout my chambers.

"Why are you weaving spells here?" I asked, perplexed and slightly shaken with today's events.

"Skuld is placing a knotting spell. This will encourage her ability to develop through her dreams. We don't have the luxury of time." Urd said.

Moira's blanched expression revealed a sadness that tore at the fibers of my heart. Tired of waiting for answers, I roared a thunderous growl of frustration.

Each woman ceased their spell making and looked at me.

Moira reached for my hand and entangled her fingers with mine.

"After the lunar eclipse and Grace's transformation is complete, she will become immortal with the ancient knowledge of the gods." Moira tilted her head back and looked into my eyes.

"What are you saying?" I pleaded with a desperation seeping inside me at the responsibilities laid upon us.

"The kundalini dragon represents the human experiment, and Grace's leadership is crucial in bringing in a new age," Verdandi said.

"Where do I fit in?"

"The fates sent you, leader of the watchers and protector of humanity, to guide the nephilim."

"I understand."

"Carman and the coven of witches want Grace's light, her power, and her knowledge of hidden magic," Urd said.

"Beware of treachery."

Skuld's haunting tone alarmed me.

She continued to weave more wards of protection around Grace's chambers. "The magical desire her light. The shifters need her power. And the gods fear her knowledge," Verdandi said.

Clenching my fist, I could feel the fury's pulse within me. Before we could find our way out of the first one, another crisis had arrived, knocking on my door. I wanted time to woo Grace and make her fall in love with me in order to go to the Olympian pantheon and bring back the sacral carnelian gem.

Moira bowed her head, and a tear slipped into the sigil ward of fae magic, binding her emotions into the weave.

"What worries you, Moira?" Urd asked.

She glanced toward Skuld and nodded before continuing with her wards.

"Carman, the Celtic witch, and her sons will escape Niflheim," Skuld said.

I wasn't quite getting the connection. I vaguely remembered something regarding a witch in Moira's past.

A tear fell on Moira's cheek. "She's my mother, a very evil sorceress. My three brothers are necromancers. Carman possesses the ancient grimoire of ley lines and dark magic."

"Okay." I was still attempting to draw logical reasoning from their words.

"I should have killed her when I had the chance." Moira pounded her fist into her other hand like a catcher does waiting for the pitcher to throw the ball.

I looked to Skuld for information.

Her hands fell to her side, and she went to Moira. "Killing your mother would have darkened your soul." Skuld faced me, and the corner of her mouth lifted. "Carman can project her essence with the help of the warlock."

"How dangerous is this woman?" I asked.

"My best friend Brigit claims she once destroyed the complete food supply in Ireland until her capture by the white sorceress Be'chulille." Moira said.

"She tricked Freyr, a Norse god, and bid him impregnate her." Urd cackled.

A shiver ran up my spine.

I tilted up Moira's chin to face me. "Dry your eyes before Uriel assumes I've caused you harm." I kissed her forehead and closed my eyes, feeling her pain.

My communicator beeped. "Gavin, what's up?"

"Flash to dock eight. Poseidon's shot through the whirlpool and is riding the waves, creating quite a stir amongst the cadets."

Just what I needed, the Greek god of the seas crashing my dinner party. I slid my fingers through my hair. "Ladies, will you join the others in the hall for drinks? Poseidon's arrived and will need to speak with me."

Skuld chuckled. "I'd expect Odin and a few of the others will arrive. Everyone will remember this great night for a myrioi of years.

"That's one powerful little wolf," I said.

"She is now, greet the all-knowing fathers, for their patience wanes thin if kept waiting."

Another blare and I flashed to the docking station in time to see the Sumerian water god, Enki, step out in a fine silk shirt, sports coat, and dark Armenia slacks. Quite the contrast to Poseidon in his chainmail and trident. "Welcome."

Another twenty water gods from all over the pantheons arrived.

Chapter Fourteen

ANANIEL

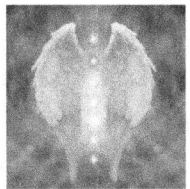

Tonight was supposed to be a small family dinner, and now gods, witches, and wolves have joined the festivities. Ready to enter the dining hall, I struggled to gather a coherent sentence in my head and failed. My whole body thrummed with excitement at meeting veritable gods. I turned to Ananiel. "How do I look?"

"Like sparkling diamonds of light."

The amused crinkle of his brow made me laugh. "Such a romantic."

Ananiel squeezed my right hand tight, leaned into me. "Do you have any of Moira's potion bites?" he asked.

"Inside my purse."

"Eat one."

"Okay." I unwrapped a piece of caramel, put it in my mouth, and waited for my body to relax. The candy took the edge off my frayed nerves.

The double doors opened onto a stunning transformation of the eating hall. I clasp my hand over my mouth. An orange glow bathed every part of the room. Thousands of gems from the table candelabra center-pieces danced in the flickering light. Terrarium orbs hung from the ceiling, filling the space with an enchantment of the Elfin realm. A viridian rug circled the floor. The tables lined the outer edges, and against the far wall, a slideshow of images presented Greek, Nordic, Sumerian, Celestial and other pantheons.

Jeffrey went to a lot of trouble.

As I entered, the music stopped, and everyone's gaze found mine.

Lowering my shoulders, I plastered on that picture-perfect smile and acknowledged our guests.

Waiting for Ananiel to walk me to the table, I stood inside the doorway. "Madam President." Jeffrey offered me a glass of red wine.

"Thanks."

Ananiel took a shot of whiskey from the tray. "Deliver a bottle to my brothers' table. I'd like to introduce them to Grace.

The eccentric bow ties didn't make me laugh aloud. The men's humorous personalities created an adorable farcical picture. "Grace, these rowdy angels are my brothers, Zadkiel, Gabriel, Rafael,..."

Jeffrey held up a bottle of Irish whiskey for Ananiel's approval.

"Good choice."

Jeffrey set five quick shot glasses in the middle of the table and then poured, leaving the bottle behind.

Luc stood to make a toast. "Hey, hey."

Ananiel narrowed his eyes at the brother with the prettiest ebony hair.

The shine from his wavy curls resembled polished onyx, almost like pure glass. My wolf's instincts perked, and I channeled a psychic awareness into the angel's persona—something I'd never done before. I could see into his heart; he carried guilt in his soul. He blamed himself for the pain he and his brothers experienced at the loss of their archeia. I didn't know how, but I saw his intention to protect his brothers, even if he had to sacrifice himself. A cool breeze prickled my skin, and a powerful protective shield dropped over his heart.

My heart went to him, and I wanted to ease his pain. Images of Ananiel rejecting his celestial home in order to stand behind Luc. I turned to the angels and saw varying shades of color around each brother and could see in their souls.

All these angels suffered in their journey to make the world a better place. I decided right then that I wanted to get to know each of them and help to ease their burdens.

"Ananiel is a person you call when you need to scare the little ones into minding their parents."

Luc's words penetrated my thoughts and brought my attention back to the room.

"His stormy nature riles the seas and challenges the gods, yet he's the most loyal of us all. He sacrificed his life for me when no other did. Ananiel is the perfect mate for the chosen silver wolf. Welcome, Grace, the sacred one."

A round of cheers went up as the entire room agreed and Led Zeppelin's "Stairway to Heaven" blared over the loud-speaker.

Uriel took his beautiful wife to the center of the room, where they danced.

Gabriel materialized his trumpet and played "Burn the House Down."

Immediately, the brothers reached for the Nephilim females and waltzed them across the floor. Lights flickered like fireflies as the women twirled with wild abandon into the prince's arms.

Ananiel took me by the hand and locked his gaze with mine.

His unfathomable magnetism drew me forward, and his warm breath fanned my cheek, sending the wildest thrill to my core.

The song died down, and everyone returned to their tables. The tables, arranged in a rectangle, allowed the guests to see one another. At the head, Yahweh, Odin, Poseidon, and many other gods each sat with a flask of something beside a silver goblet. To the right of the gods sat the Norns. Beside them sat Uriel and Moira. Roger and Dustin joined Ananiel and me. Many of Aiden's pack were here, and they intermixed with the Nephilim cadets and guardians to round out the room.

Jeffrey orchestrated the servers to place the plates on the table. A rhythm of sound filled the room, with forks clinking and crystal singing a melodic tune. In some ways, it felt like the last supper. After today, I'd return to the White House, unsure of whom to trust. Any of my associates could be in league with Norman.

I sensed Ananiel kept something from me. Tomorrow, my life changed. I could no longer pretend I wasn't part of the shifters. Soon, the American people must face their fears and realize the supernatural realm had always involved itself in American politics.

After the shift, my body was stronger, aware of sounds and smells I'd never noticed before. The intentions of were people easy to read if they didn't block their minds. Ananiel shadowed a part of his heart after the sexual frenzy last night. I wasn't sure if he could accept me as a mate.

Gabriel blew his trumpet, and the conversations silenced.

Yahweh and the other three gods rose.

"Grace, stand before us," Yahweh said.

Ananiel took my hand, and we flashed to the center rectangle.

Regaining my balance, I trembled inside, not sure what to expect. As I faced four powerful gods, my intuitive instincts flew out the window. I was President of the United States, but at this moment, my title seemed like a minor accomplishment amidst these men.

Ananiel flashed back to his seat, leaving me alone. Endless questions bombarded my thoughts, and I wondered why the gods of the pantheons wanted me to face them like a panel of judges ready to pass retribution.

Yahweh filled a goblet with red wine and moved around the table to face her in the center of the room. "The wine of the gods. Each of us will gift the silver wolf with a power from our pantheon to use only once in a time of great peril. Think and use them wisely."

A golden light shimmered around him, drawing me in his circle of light. A musical tenor filled the room, blocking out all other sensations.

"I gift you with the ability to make life-or-death decisions. Use this gift with wisdom, for every choice, even made for the right reason, has consequences."

I took the goblet, brought the fruity wine to my lips, and sipped.

Odin rose and filled my goblet from his flask. "This mead protects your flesh from harm. Illness will no longer affect you. Your body will easily repair when wounded. A touch of your hand in times of need will heal those in great distress. Keep your spirit pure, and your skills will save many in the future. I gift you with one chance to open the portal and free one soul to save a life. Use it wisely."

I swallowed the mead, and the aches of yesterday disappeared. The hanging lights flickered, and the room grew dim. The hair on my body reacted as a magnetic force reorganized my cells, leaving me tingling with energy.

Poseidon rose and poured from a cockleshell. "Drink the nectar. The power of the elements will guide you on the journey facing the evil magic that threatens to tarnish the light. In your time of greatest peril, call any of the Greek gods, and we'll assist you in your need."

I emptied the goblet, and tears of gratitude filled my eyes.

Enki rose, holding a golden horn. "The magic of color is yours to use in your time of need. Beware of gray, for that color enhances what one fears."

A kaleidoscope of the rainbow whirled in my mind. Speechless, I swallowed hard. My nerves were as fragile as tree roots holding precariously to a storm-ravaged island. I silently called for Ananiel because, at the moment, my legs were cement, unable to move.

His warm hands touched my lower back, and we flashed back to our seats. He reached into his pocket and handed me a caramel bite.

Desperate to calm my nerves, I grabbed the candy and popped it into my mouth. "Thanks."

The rest of the evening drifted like floating clouds. My thoughts remained in a fog. Soon, I'd return to the White House a completely different woman.

"Are you coming with me when I go home?" I asked Ananiel, feeling vulnerable. My wolf wanted to mark him and establish his role in my life. I also wanted him to love me and surrender because he wanted to, not because it was our destiny.

"Depends. Don't worry, I've arranged for the Nordic wolves, Juna, and the cadets to see to your safety. They will be part of your new security team."

"I see. Juna and her team will be a great addition to my staff." I hid the disappointment snaking through my stomach like acid ready to strike.

The party wound down, and people returned to their quarters or ventured around the island.

Ananiel reached for my hand and flashed us back to his rooms.

I wanted to argue, but in reality, I was exhausted. My emotions, like a rollercoaster going backwards, were all over the place. The Aiden packmaster agreed to allow me to choose a mate from within the group, but my heart wasn't interested. Ananiel was someone I wanted to really love me.

How did he feel about the frenzy? This was part of wolf culture, yet a dark sense of unease filled my heart at remembering how my mother lived as an outcast from not only her clan, but my father's people.

Aunt Cherly hated my mother, and she claimed shifters were freaks who should be hunted to extermination. Every ounce of my aunt's venom ran through my veins, making it difficult to embrace the wolf shifter within me.

Chapter Fifteen

ANANIEL

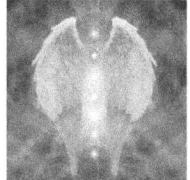

After the party, I flashed us to her bedroom.

She stood against the writing desk, clutching her fist. Her chest rose in fast little pulses, and her heartbeat thundered in my ears. I tipped up her head and kissed her goodnight. I'd felt her uncertainty regarding the frenzy and where our relationship with each other stood.

Our sigil signature that connected us together made it hard to think clearly with her emotions flooding through me. I hated causing her stress, but I needed to work things out in my mind. Regardless of her own powerful strengths, she must listen to her heart and accept me as her spirit-mate and alpha based on wolf traditions.

If at any time her wolf went rogue, I'd need to counteract the black magic, especially if the mages manipulated her god-like powers. And that meant she must accept me as her alpha and allow the exchange of blood to seal the connection. I doubted Grace, as a woman, had submitted to any man in her past. T

As I stood there like a boy on his first date, I turned toward the door waiting. I badgered myself. The idea of rejection stirred a tidal wave of storms inside my heart. I cared for her, though I tried to deny it. More than physical intimacy, I yearned for something. Marking me, I thought she would, but it didn't happen. She could claim another male if she chose.

Changing my mind about leaving, I turned and faced Grace. She still wore the emerald gown from dinner. As my fingers slid down her spine, she arched her slender back. My hand touched the buttons at her back. My body hardened at the thought of spending the night with her. I nestled my nose in her curls and inhaled the scent of her jasmine shampoo. "Will you stay with me?" My voice was a harsh whisper.

"I thought you'd never ask." She tilted her head back.

I traced my lips along the curves of her throat. "Tonight, my sweet wolf, you'll scream my name as I fill you like no other man."

"Confident, aren't you?"

I turned her toward me, pulling the top of her dress from her shoulders. I hooked a hand under her knee and hiked her leg around my waist, grazing my fingertips on the garter. Holy shit, this woman knew how to tease me into submission. "How far are you willing to go, Madam President?"

I pulled aside her panties and slipped a hand inside to find her soaking wet. My fingers entered her soft folds, and my gaze lingered on the curving line of her lips as her orgasm neared. I pulled away.

"Don't stop," she moaned.

"Take off your dress but leave on the silk stockings."

She did as she was told.

"Now, sit on the bed and open your legs." I unhooked her right stocking and slowly slid the silky fabric down her leg. I tied the stocking around her ankle then arched a brow to see if she'd agree.

"Yes." She met the heat of my gaze with her own.

This woman was wilder than I'd assumed. I tied her foot to the bedpost. Pushing her to her limits, I'd see how far I could go. "Tonight is for the wolf. She must accept me as her alpha."

"Other men wish to be my mate, what makes you so sure you're in the running?"

"Are you challenging my right?" As I inched the other silk stocking off her leg and tied her other ankle, I raked my gaze over her body.

"Until I mark my mate, the frenzy continues. You can't interfere, and I'm free to explore."

"Do you desire the others?"

Her bravado slipped, and her fingers grazed my face. "No."

I pulled out of her reach until she lowered her arms. "Accept me as your alpha."

I sensed Grace's turmoil and felt the pull of her sexual pain. A guttural growl came from her throat. The silver wolf's spirit fought to control the situation. Grace wanted to surrender, but a part of her held back as she writhed in ecstasy. My lust twisted in a way that hurt. Our sigil connection had intertwined, and I experienced every moment of frenzy and indecision that Grace did.

Spreading her knees apart, I widened her folds and touched the glistening of her pink skin.

"Stop teasing me," she cried out.

"Are you still in need of the other wolves?"

"No!" Her words came out way too fast making me doubt her honesty.

My tongue swept over her pulsing clit, and I entered two fingers inside her as she arched into my hand. I pushed harder, wanting to influence her choice and to hear my name called.

Her hands ruffled my hair, pushing my head into her wet pussy.

I lifted my head and demanded. "Choose first or no pleasure."

"I need..."

"Choose."

"No..."

A knock at the door caught my attention. "Not now." I grunted.

"It's Seth, I'm coming inside."

As I rose from my position between her legs, I heard a key turn in the lock.

Seth from the Aiden pack entered the room dressed in jeans. His shirt lay open, and he was barefoot.

Not a good sign. "What do you want?"

Seth's mouth quirked to the right as he studied the situation. He gazed at Grace and back to me. "Apparently you need my help."

I was fully clothed as Grace, in all her beauty, lay sprawled across my bed. The scent of arousal hung in the air.

The alpha's eyes narrowed.

I sensed his reaction to her. Every nerve in my body shrieked to get to him and make him leave.

"The silver wolf appears to need a lesson in shifter wolf submission." His fingers tugged on the silk stocking, and his tongue traced his lower lip.

Her eyes widened in desire.

Part of me wanted to demand he leave, but I understood that if she didn't choose, the shifter nation stood to suffer great losses. The sacral chakra was the base of sexuality and energy. "Do you want him to watch, or do you prefer he touch you?"

"Umm, I don't know."

"Yes, you do. What do you want?" I demanded. My emotions were at their limit. I had no intention of sleeping with her until she chose. If it meant another night of the frenzy, I'd agree. Roger warned me that the frenzy usually lasted seven days before the female chose her mate. Another week would break my spirit.

"I won't be rushed," she stated as she lowered her arms to cover her exposed breasts.

The alpha of the Aiden pack smiled as he reached over and kissed Grace's mouth. "You are a sweet one. Which of us will you choose tonight? The marking must be done to calm the packs soon.

Her hand slid over his bare chest and stopped at the top of his trousers.

I fought back the need to kill him. No matter the fates, if she wanted him this night, I'd step away.

She turned to me. "I want you both."

Only one of us would carry her mark in the morning. Between her spread legs, I on one side and he the other, our hands edged along her inner thighs. Together, we opened the folds to her flesh. Her skin glistened with wetness as we both entered our fingers into her pussy. She moaned.

I felt the confusion and conflict within her heart. Wanting to fight the pleasure, she needed to ease the frenzy. I removed my fingers, as did Seth. He appeared to be following my lead, and we both walked to my room, allowing her time to decide without our influence.

Chapter Sixteen

ANANIEL

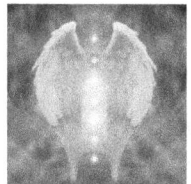

"Gentleman, come back in here." Grace leaned against the backboard of the bed. I waited, feeling the deep, heated desire of emotion in her soul. Would she want me? An angel unworthy of her, she'd be better off with the alpha leader.

She gazed between the two of us. "Before I decide, both of you will surrender allegiance to each other. The dark days ahead will require we band together. The pantheons will need everyone doing their part."

She was right, but I wanted her for my own. Sharing her even in this way bothered me. Her heart was pure, and I felt her desire for me, but then, the others arrived, and her sexual needs overshadowed logic. If she chose the alpha wolf, I would see them to the surface and return as a failure.

"I pledge my loyalty to the Aiden pack." I reached out my hand and Seth shook it.

"The pack respects all you have sacrificed, Sarim prince. We pledge our loyalty to the celestial pantheon."

She gazed at Seth and then toward me, as if playing us both like a violin.

I tossed her one of my shirts. "Would you like a shot of whiskey?" I asked Seth.

He, too, got up and followed me into my own personal chamber. We were both fully dressed and aware of the game taking place.

"The next few weeks will be dangerous. A new development has occurred since we last spoke," I said, lowering my voice to prevent Grace from hearing our conversation. I poured two shots, and we downed them.

Seth motioned toward Grace's room. "She's a tough one. I know she wants you, it was apparent in the way she reacts to your touch. Why does she hold back?"

"She's used to going it alone." I poured another shot, and we sat in the arm-chairs of my study.

"There's more?" Seth said, rubbing the bristly hairs on his chin. "She's hiding. Why?"

"She's frightened and fights her destiny." I looked toward her room, hearing her rustle around inside before the sound of the shower started.

"We're out of time. She must choose, or I'll be forced to take her against her will." Seth stirred, a slight ripple of muscle warning of his enormous strength. A protector of his pack.

The tendons in my neck tightened, making my words difficult to say. "No one takes her by force."

"Then make sure she brands you with her mark tonight," he snapped and slammed his fist onto the table.

"Why the urgency?" I asked him, taking a swig of whiskey.

"Turmoil between the supernaturals and the human government rises. Blood was spilled this morning. The shifters fear for their children and wives." He rose and filled our glasses. "Hunters are tracking shifters."

I rose and faced him. "What happened?" My tone resonated with an alpha challenge.

Seth placed a hand on my shoulder. "Today, two shifter towns were burnt to the ground. Several children were trapped inside a school house." and his voice quivered, broke then became strong.

"What did the paranormal agency do?" I shifted my feet and walked to the portal that opened to the sea.

"They've demanded the arrest of the culprits, but in reality, the shifters fear the humans won't carry out the law."

"They're probably right." I gazed out to the sea, watching the schools of fish hustle by. The situation escalated, and the shifters needed hope.

"Your archeia must accept her destiny. Time has run out."

"Tonight she will choose."

Seth joined me at the window. He paused. "Make sure she does."

"Had her brothers nurtured her in the shifter pack ways, this decision would be easier, but she's lived within the human belief system with small glimpses of her supernatural identity. She's suppressed her wolf since childhood."

"If times were different, I'd never have knocked on your door." Seth mouth tightened. "We don't have time to allow the cycle to play out. Grace needs to mark her chosen before she returns to the White House, or the other tribes will not follow her lead."

"We've given her an ultimatum. Let her scramble with her decision."

"I'm leaving at sunset tomorrow. My friend, I expect to see you marked.

I assume you are comfortable.

"The accommodations surpass my expectations."

"Another?"

Without saying a word to either of us, she left my home. I could only guess where she might be going. The rumbles of anxiety stirred throughout her body, and I wanted to go to her and offer comfort, but I must not until she decided.

"Did you really intend to take her as a mate?" I asked once Grace was gone.

"She is not mine. And besides, I have an alpha female I'm interested in. Her shift occurred last year, and I carry her mark."

Seth cut me a hard look that said he hated betraying his own lover. "Why haven't you completed the mating ritual?" I should leave this matter alone, but I wanted to understand his willingness to deny his own desires for the good of his pack.

"I am alpha, and until the silver wolf comes into her own, I've no right to indulge in my desire. Should Grace request I take her as mate, I will have little choice but to sacrifice the one I love. Our packs must survive."

"She is my archeia, but for the kundalini dragon to rise, she must fall in love with me before the lunar eclipse during the night of the full moon."

Seth chuckled and poured us both another shot of the whiskey. "The blood festival is a sacred night in the shifter world. Your brother's mentioned a curse and a bet between your gods. How does it relate to the silver wolf?"

"My brothers and I fought in the great celestial wars between Diablo and Yahweh for control over the mortals. A group of angels confronted the all-father, Yahweh, for dominance. In his anger, Yahweh banished the angels from Kumuria, our celestial home." The memories cooked in the juices of his resentment like a cancer gnawing on his last nerve.

"And were you cast out?"

We settled back into the arm-chairs, more relaxed now that the whiskey hit the blood stream. Angels had an extremely high metabolism rate, and it took far more than four shots to render me incapable of functioning.

"Not in the beginning. When my mother followed my elder brother to the mortal world, I spoke up against our father. His own pride wouldn't allow him to bend to my mother's pleas not to banish Lucifer to live among the demons."

Seth's jaw tightened. "Was the punishment deserved?"

"Luc was the leader of the angels. He challenged our father and lost."

"In the wolf pack, Lucifer would have been banished just the same. Once an ultimatum is given there can be only be one winner. Why did you leave?"

"Our father, in his rage, forced our souls to divide. The Sarim princes' archeia females died instantly, to be reborn in other pantheons."

"Harsh." A muscle jumped in his jaw.

I removed the dress shirt I still wore. Underneath my left pectoral muscle, the fishhook scar festered red. The wound got worse each day. If Grace rejected me as her mate, the kundalini would die, leaving a severe rip in the fabric of the universe.

"Do you love her?" Seth eyed me and paused, crossing his legs.

"I recognize my archeia in Grace, but do I love her? I don't know." So much had happened with the attempt on her life.

"Fair enough answer."

"I've been angry for a long time, and bitterness tarnishes one's soul." I spared a glance toward the closed door.

"Love can save one's heart."

"Even you are willing to sacrifice love for the pack. I clearly see Grace means little to you except for her role as the silver wolf." My temper riled, I rose and opened Grace's door. I just stood looking into her rooms.

Seth stood beside me, and we both stared at the rumpled bed. "The silver wolf has been foretold for hundreds of years. Her story passed down through the generations that one day a wolf would rise to unite all the tribes into a cohesive unit." He settled his long, lean body against the doorframe.

He was right, Grace had to choose. Exhaustion underscored the dark shadows under Seth's eyes. "Get some rest. I'll speak with you before the days end."

"Make her submit, my friend. She is our only hope."

I turned away and glanced out the window, unwilling to reveal the fear soaring in my heart. If she rejected me all was lost. After I swallowed the lump in my throat, I faced Seth. "I'll speak with you before you leave."

We shook hands and Seth left.

Taking a deep breath of courage, I flashed to the estuary.

Chapter Seventeen

GRACE

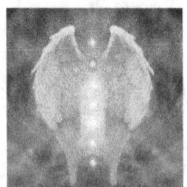

Wrapped in Ananiel's shirt, I breathed in his brine scent. The scent was of the sea and the man I was falling in love with. I sat huddled inside a secluded alcove right above the cave, knowing he'd find me. I respected his giving me space and honoring my need to make my choice.

Hearing my mother's dying words: *Hide your wolf and keep the locket hidden.* I shivered. I clasped my fingers around the Viking triquetra my mother gave me right before my parents' tragic deaths. Now I was exposed, and mages wanted my magic, which meant I would have to lead the shifters in their protest against the tyranny of the mortal realm. Once the humans learned of my shifter nature, I'd be every zealot's target.

Yesterday, I'd wanted to leave. Now, watching my future collide with my past didn't sound like fun, but if I didn't return to the White House, the shifters had little chance of protecting their rights as citizens. I soaked in the mystic energy of the land.

In less than a week, I'd complete my transition. Usually, the pack held a ceremonial festival honoring the claiming between couples. When Ananiel tossed me his shirt, I was grateful for his understanding. Somewhere in the depths of my heart, I loved the sacrifices he made for me.

Thinking of Ananiel's powerful arms wrapped around me made me whimper. I wanted him. The crunching sound of twigs caught my attention.

"Grace."

His tone was gentle and coaxing, like he was talking to a trapped animal. In some ways, I was. I feared my wolf and the expectations the supernaturals had for me. More twigs crackled. "I'm over here."

Ananiel pulled back the branch of a hedge maple.

I was crouched with my knees against my chest, wearing his shirt and a pair of leggings. I cupped my fingers and gave him a wave. His mouth was full, with a touch of harshness that I ached to kiss.

"Having fun?" He arched his brow.

"Actually, I am. Are you aware of how many insects fly around at night?"

His laughter lightened the tension.

He sat beside me. "Why don't you inform me?"

"Well, I've seen love bugs, gnats, and cooties."

"Love bugs, never heard of them."

"You know, the bugs whose bodies stay connected for days after mating. Now, that's some wild sex going on. Almost as crazy as the wolf's frenzy."

"Are you okay?" he asked with a hint of concern.

My gaze swept across the seashore and into the moon's orange hues. "I'm sorry about tonight."

His silence spoke volumes. I'd been right, Ananiel's only concern was ending my transition and returning me to the surface. My throat closed at the thought of choosing another, but Seth was right. The wolves needed a mated leader to follow.

He took my hand in his and flashed us back to his bedroom. "I've never allowed a woman to come in here, but tonight, you will submit to me."

I detected a spark of mischief in his voice. He played with a tendril of my hair lying on my sensitive neck.

Shivers of delight hit my core, and I thought I'd explode if he didn't make love to me.

"Not so fast, my sexual wolf. We've unfinished business. Now, where were we before Seth interrupted us?"

His breath tickled my shoulder, and I offered him my neck.

"That's it, lean back into me."

His fingers undid each button in agonizing slowness, making me want to scream. With each success, he nibbled my neck. His hand cupped my left breast, making me squirm.

"Ananiel." I reached for him.

"Do not orgasm until I give you permission."

Everywhere he touched me, felt as if an electrical current pulsed beneath my skin. I could hear, see, smell, taste, and feel him. Fire I'd never imagined seared my feminine center. My wolf howled her joy within my mind. This is the man she and I would mate. Her alpha.

He pinched my nipple making it as hard as a sharp dagger point.

"Yes, baby. Make those nipples stand up for me." He pinched the other one.

I gasp.

I reached up and fisted a handful of his hair, crying his name.

"Not yet." He captured my hand in his and brought my arm to my side. After he released the last button and removed my leggings, he spread the lips of my labia and entered one finger, swirling in my hot juices.

His lips continued down my shoulder and across my arm. I felt his body pull away from mine leaving me empty. He removed his shirt and dropped it to the floor. His massive cock tented his slacks. A cock I wanted in my mouth, and my body.

He stared as if he were photographing me with his eyes. The power and strength radiating from him sent pleasure to my core. My mouth watered, and I reached for his belt. His eyes grew golden, and a fire flickered within. Not waiting another second, I released his manhood and climbed to my knees. Blood pounded in my brain with the sensual heat sizzling through me.

"Holy fuck."

Ananiel palmed the back of my head as I swallowed his cock, enjoying his feel. He tried to pull out, but I'd have none of it. If he wanted submission, then he'd have to submit to me before I gave myself over to him. I wanted no other man. Ananiel was my mate and, damn it to hell, I'd make him break first. I kneaded his buttocks, and my excitement grew at the groans coming from him. Before the night was over, we'd experienced each other to the fullest.

I lowered my hand over his butt cheeks and squeezed. My mouth was a hot, wet oven for his release.

"I'm coming. I can't stop." His voice was feral, brutish in his heat.

I swallowed his seed and flattened my tongue under the sensitive tip, coaxing every drop. My hands lowered to grip his forearms. His fingers pulled my hair as he continued to spasm. My canines lengthened, and my wolf punctured his thigh to claim him by leaving my mating mark.

His fingers released my hair as he gently caressed my shoulder. Laughter barreled out of him as I relaxed my grip on his skin. "That's one way to claim me."

I saw the relief in his eyes.

I'd chosen him.

Chapter Eighteen

ANANIEL

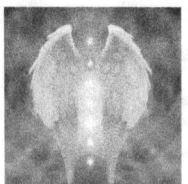

I collapsed, covering her body like a thermal blanket. She'd given me the best orgasm of my life. Never had a woman taken me so fully into her being. What started out as an act of making her submit backfired under her skillful, hungry kiss.

As soon as I caught my breath, I'd have her in every position and make her scream my name over and over until she couldn't utter another sound. I flashed and brought us back to our apartment.

I reached into my nightstand and brought out packages of condoms. The last thing we needed was for her to become pregnant.

Her eyes widened as I also pulled out lavender-rose oil. A massage was a perfect way to learn every curve of her sexy body.

"Can I orgasm now?" she asked, pouting her kissable lips.

"Not yet." I kissed her beautiful mouth.

She'd submitted and willingly waited. Her emotions slithered around my body, filling me with her lust. She wanted more. The intensity of her pulse and the pounding of her heart filled me with power.

I rubbed her cheek, running my fingers across her adorable mouth. "Before the night is through, I will make you come so many times that you won't be able to move." I reached down and lifted her to the bed.

My lips brushed against her wet mouth. "You will submit your entire body, mind, and soul to me," I whispered in her ear.

She quivered as her tongue snaked its way over her bottom lip. Her body arched into me.

I captured her mouth, pulling and suckling. The kiss was like the soldering heat that melds metal with each other. My erection pushed against her belly needing to possess her, but I'd wait.

"Take me right now."

Her voice flowed over me like honey: teasing, sticky and sweet.

I slid from the bed and took out a scarf from my drawer. "I'm blind-folding you. Are you all right with that?"

A look of indecision wavered in her green eyes as she contemplated me. "Is this another act of control to make me surrender to your dominance?"

"I am your alpha. Trust me in all things. When we face the mages, you might need to use your sensory perception to identify the world around you."

"And blindfolding me will teach me to be aware?"

"Do you trust me?" I left the scarf in her lap.

"Debating." She took it in her hand. "I have a condition of my own."

"I'm listening."

"When my transition's complete and the warlock is subdued, I want you to take me on a first date."

My heart reached out to her. None of the sex had been about love, but submission. Yes, I'd take her on all the dates she wanted once the kundalini rose.

She tossed me an uncertain look.

"Yes, I promise you a special first date."

"I also want to get married in a church, which differs from Angel or Wolf traditions, but I've always dreamed of a wedding like most little girls."

My brows rose, and I felt like she threw me a curve-ball that kept going in circles.

"Wolves don't have church weddings. They mate and have a

bonding ritual." I rubbed my palm across the back of my neck, deliberating what direction to take this conversation.

"I'll choose for the pack, but I won't complete the ritual without the promise of a human wedding."

Her emotions leaked out like water through her fingers, and I felt her slip from me. Needing a moment, I stepped into the next room to retrieve a tray of food and drink that I had Jeffrey deliver while I'd gone to find Grace.

Grace's beautiful dark hair, streaked with silver, made me ache with desire. The events of the evening still surprised me. After Seth joined us, I was positive she'd select one wolf. Her lust for Seth shredded my heart, but I'd deal with my feelings another time. Tonight was about her submission, and her learning to trust without restraints.

I needed to push her to the limit and test all her boundaries. Grace, for her own welfare, had to trust me with her whole being, not only her words. The dangers facing us were grim.

I held out a glass of chardonnay.

She threw her legs over the side of the bed and gave me a soft caress with her gaze. "I trust you."

"Trust me enough to surrender in all things to hear my commands and heed my voice."

"Yes." She sipped at her wine.

Our sigil tie tightened around my heart. If the warlock stole her essence, I'd kill every witch in the earthly realm.

"Your stormy eyes match the raging sea of Poseidon. I see why he protects your island."

"I'm a creature of the sea its power speaks to me and through me."

"What thoughts ventured through your mind causing your pupils to darken in rage?"

"The mere thought of the warlock harming you makes my anger rise like a fiery inferno." After swigging the shot, I set the glass on the table.

"I require a suitcase filled with Moira's Caramels.

"I'll let her know."

"Stormy."

"What?"

"Stormy's my safe word. Stormy reminds me of you, with your furious energy and your wild streak."

She brushed her curvy, sizzling body against mine. I took the cloth and wrapped it around her eyes.

A hint of resistance surged through her system before her tension subsided, and she leaned closer.

"Lie down on your stomach." Grace sat the glass on the night stand and crawled into bed.

I lifted her foot, massaging the arch, then I moved up her legs, spreading them wide. Her beautiful, sweet pussy called, and I wanted to experience her tight folds around me.

"That feels good," she murmured.

I moved my hands to her back, massaging the rose oil into her skin. My hard cock throbbed as I rubbed my shaft between her warm butt cheeks. I poured oil over her puckered opening, determined I'd fill every one of her holes before the night was finished. Her wolf's frenzy grew and became stronger. A growl came from her throat as her nails tightened into the sheets. I knew she still experienced the transition.

"Do you need the others?" I asked, dreading her answer.

"I desire only my alpha."

At those words, I plunged my cock into her hard and fast. Her sweet pussy gloved me like a perfect fit. So tight and warm.

"More," she screamed.

I pushed my thumb inside her anus. She arched her back and cried out as her orgasm crested.

Removing my hand from her bottom, I gripped her thighs, leaned over her back and bit her shoulder, claiming her in the traditional custom of the mating frenzy. Her blood tingled my tongue. The sigil signature circle opened, and I sensed even more of her spirit. The sensation flooded me, and I came, filling her with everything I had.

Our breaths shallow, I slid my hand over the scarf and removed it.

Her beautiful green eyes looked into mine and she murmured the words I needed to hear.

"My chosen."

"My archeia." I mumbled, kissing the nape of her neck.

The frenzy was over, and I collapsed, relieved that this powerful woman had chosen me.

Chapter Nineteen

ANANIEL

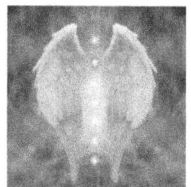

Grace's soft snores drew my attention. Her submission deflated the clouds of discomfort within my soul. With the surrender of my archeia, the claiming gave the sigil spell a powerful boost. Not only could I experience her feelings, but I could see her thoughts if she didn't block them. I'll have to teach her how the angels block each other from ease dropping when we want privacy.

Her cute cupid lips twitched right as her eyes fluttered open.

A wicked curve formed around her mouth. "Morning, Alpha."

"Madam President."

Our gazes locked, reading the other's unspoken words. Last night changed the game. She'd accepted me. I savored the glide of her silken skin under my palm. Neither of us wanted to rise from our cocoon of warm sleep.

Jeffrey knocked three times, informing me that many of my guest were stirring throughout the guild. The last thing I wanted was to leave my bed, but I needed to privately meet with Seth and the Aiden pack before their evening departure.

As her nails raked across my abdomen, gooseflesh tingled along my spine. Her slender fingers circled the trident marking she'd left on my inner thigh. My cock throbbed hard in her hand, and I gasped for breath.

"Allow me to enjoy my mighty sea angel."

Her words echoed in my thoughts as she tugged at the sigil signature spell that wove our two bodies together. Her new powers twisted within me as the wolf's essence dominated Grace.

I rose to my knees and let her to take me deep inside her mouth. Moans escaped me as she claimed domination over my body. "Take what you need."

I gripped her shoulders as my cock hit the back of her throat, enjoying every stroke of her tongue. Unable to take the pressure another moment, I slid from her grasp. Flipping her over, I saw my own trident symbol materialized on her right shoulder. "Open for me and take the power of the sea inside you."

A jaunty laugh escaped her as if she were riding the wind and I were her slave. She was as eager and erratic as a summer storm. I intended to savor every ounce of her nature.

"Ananiel."

As she called my name, I tingled, and the rage of passion crested like the white caps of the evening tide. Her body clenched me in orgasmic thrall hurtling me beyond the point of no return.

I curled behind Grace, keeping her spooned against me. Once we left this room, the next forty-eight hours threatened to sweep my archeia from my reach, back into a world of political strife between humans who lacked the foresight to keep her safe.

"Aqapai," I whispered into the side of her neck. My beautiful Grace belonged to the people of the supernatural and mortal realms. The silver wolf's rise to power was humanity's hope for a brighter future.

"You are my lifeline, my mate."

I tightened my arm around her waist, pulling her against my chest. I felt trepidation ripple through her body. "You'll be fine."

A sigh released from her. "You're not going with me are you?"

Her sharp tone caused me to grimace.

"I have other obligations that demand attention."

"Why not?"

"I have my own journey to accomplish. I'm meant to locate the sacral carnelian scarab and together you and I will return the gem to the kundalini dragon."

"What's happening in the White House?"

"Our spies report that your double is vacationing at Cape Cod and will return to the White House Monday morning."

As her anxiety soared through her blood stream, our sigil connection slammed into me. "What the fuck!" I slid from our bed, unable to deal with the powerful misgivings that surged through her.

Her fear hurt me. Leaving her alone and scared caused the turbulent seas to wreak havoc on the surface as I fought the rage pulling at my soul.

I lifted Grace into my arms and held her close. "I promise you I'll return as soon as possible." I kissed her and wiped away the tears forming in her eyes. "I've got a great idea."

"What?" The tension eased from her shoulders and she melded into my embrace

"Dress for a workout. After brunch with Moira and Uriel, I'd like to see you fight with your security team."

She stopped at the bathroom door. "I'm not ready."

I arched my brow unsure of what she meant. "You're the president, the legendary silver wolf."

"With the gods' gift of power, can I, despite my inexperience, truly defeat a seasoned warlock?"

"We'll work on your strengths. Any new talents?"

"Telekinesis." Interesting side effect, not a skill I expected. "Turn the shower on without touching the knobs."

Grace and I walked into the bathroom. I watched her eyes turn a light shamrock shade, and she concentrated on the task. I joined her when she stepped into the glass enclosure. In a moment, warm water spouted from the jets, and a bubble of joy rose from her, making me hug her close.

"Let's not waste it." I trapped her arms against the tile wall as the water pelted my back.

I stepped out of the shower and handed her a towel. "Here's my private chute to the surface. I'll program it to open inside the presidential suite. If you need to escape, use it. It will transport you immediately to Archipelago Island.

"That's nifty. And when do you plan to use your private entrance?"

"Soon as possible," I chuckled, determined to lighten the heaviness in the room.

A bugle sound blasted from my phone, Gabriel's way of warning me that the eleven princes were about to break into my quarters. "Dress quickly; my brothers will be here soon."

"Come out after you finish dressing."

"We're here." Zadkiel, the Dominion leader, and one of the eldest opened the door as they all collided into the room. "And so is Father."

Crimson light filled the room in contrast with the dark blue flame burning in my blood. I stiffened my spine. He'd come yesterday, but not once had he been to the island to visit the hybrid nephilim before now. He blamed the Grigori watchers for mating with mortal females. Had the watchers not gathered the Nephilim descendants and trained them as guardians, the lechers of magic would have used the demigods to inflict horrible grievances on humankind.

Yahweh in his grand appearance filled my office doorway. He wore a royal purple breastplate, covering his muscular frame. The red dragon emblem across his sash symbolized my mother's origins from the ancient Sumerians. The betrayal settled deep inside me, as if I remembered yesterday when they cast away our archeias. What right did he have to mourn her? That she left to live out her immortality in the human realm was his fault.

Grace opened the bedroom door. All conversation seized.

The tension in the room radiated a volcanic heat, waiting for a match to strike and ignite the explosion.

As Yahweh approached me, my brothers scattered against the wall. Moira entered the room and rescued Grace.

My father stood inches from me. "You've done a fine job in protecting the nephilim."

His words were slow in coming. Because of your anger, you abandoned our children. You forsake your sons to live without our mates. Without mercy, you demand obedience. And you expect me to roll over and accept your praise?" I couldn't afford to care or indulge myself in emotions. They would lead to disaster. Father had his own agenda regarding the effect on any of the angel realms.

"The Grigori watchers, like you my son have played a vital role in human affairs. Release your resentment and embrace your destiny."

Gabriel and Zadkiel each placing a hand on my shoulder. Zadkiel, spoke to us all.

"The Nephilim are part of the dilemma facing the magical, shifters, and humans." Gabe's words echoed across the room. "A war of magic is on the horizon."

"What do the Nephilim have to do with magic? They're children of angels and protectors of humans."

Gabriel's tone grew cold and certain. "The necromancers, the coven of witches, the shifter hunters, and the gods of the elementals of the underworld realms threaten the balance of the universe."

The storm brewing between the veils of darkness and light weighed heavy on the five Sarim princes. If any of the angels failed, a sinister era like none had seen would enslave the pantheons. I sighed.

Grace, my beautiful Grace, must bring the supernaturals and the humans together to prevent those cast out from the symphony of light from bringing the dissonance of evil.

"The mortal realm is close to extinction because of its poverty, politics, and petty wars. Because of this, humans find themselves integrated with shifters and magical pantheons. Soon, supernaturals will return the world to glory." Yahweh bellowed, as if talking to an arena of soldiers, not his sons. "The Nephilim will be elite warriors and leaders of men, helping to bring in a new world order on Earth."

"You cared little for our off spring in the past. Why the sudden respect for the Grigori watchers and their young?"

"Ananiel, your insolence demeans you. Destiny required that you defy me. If Lucifer hadn't challenged my authority, humankind would have perished, leaving a void in the universe."

His words silenced me while I gathered another reason to thwart him. "And losing our mother to the material mortal world?"

"Her departure was unexpected."

"If you hadn't banished Luc from Kumuria, none of us would have suffered such agony."

"Your pain prepared you for the next pantheon war."

I begrudgingly gazed into the crimson light of my father and bowed in subservience, accepting Yahweh's divine grace.

"You gotta be kidding. Never did I think Ananiel would return to the fold," Gabriel stuttered, his eyebrows jerking upward at my calm appearance.

I, like my brothers, wanted the return of our archeia.

"I haven't. Don't mistake my compliance for forgiveness," I snarled in a gruff tone. "Until our mother returns to Kumuria, I will always live within the earthly plane."

"At least it's a compromise," Zadkiel stated.

I detected a spark of mischief in his voice, letting me know he understood what it took for me to bow to our father.

Yahweh dimmed his bright light. "My greatest regret is allowing your mother to leave. I, too, want the kundalini to rise and bring home my family to Kumuria."

I heard the hurt and pain in his voice. The hardness around my heart softened, feeling my father's agony over the loss of his Shekina.

Chapter Twenty

NORMAN

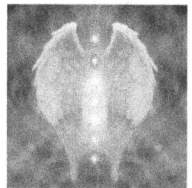

I studied the building, the exits and entrances. Who entered and when? A rational plan formed in my mind. In a couple of days, twenty regional alphas would arrive in D.C. If I timed my next move correctly, I'd wipe out half the alpha leaders in one swoop, leaving the packs scrambling for leadership.

Next, as payment for losing Grace, I'd blame the incident on her brothers. I still couldn't believe she lived. If my information was correct, I risked her reappearing at the White House—but I'd be ready. A righteous satisfaction swelled in me. As rogue alpha wolves, they'd be rejected in both worlds. If Grace tried to prove our innocence, she'd have to expose herself. Grace would pay for denying me my revenge. I'd still have her, but she'd lose everyone she loved.

"Norm."

I turned and walked back inside, closing the sliding glass doors. My sister Sheila stood in my office. "Look at my new doll."

"She's beautiful. What's her name?"

"Dotty."

Her eyes sparkled with childish glee. At twenty-nine, she was a shell of her former self, her bright mind lost in darkness after the horrible rape of her magic and body.

I had promised to destroy every wolf shifter and their offspring. Just this morning, hunters notified me that two shifter camps in upper Wyoming were burned to the ground. I would make sure not one wolf shifter survived for what happened to my sister. I lived for nothing more than to kill those I hated—and I hated the wolves. I hoped Grace would return, making my revenge even sweeter. She'd be surprised at what I had planned.

"Go back to watching television. Your nanny will play with you."

"Kay." She shuffled off into the living room, leaving me to my thoughts.

I went to the liquor cabinet, poured a fresh bourbon, and returned to the balcony. If only my magick were powerful enough to turn back time. I would sacrifice my riches to return to that horrific afternoon when I'd found three shifters squatting beside her torn body.

A cold hand grazed my shoulder. Carman's imprint sent a shiver through me. She projected her essence from Niflheim, the land of the dead where Odin kept her prisoner. The Celtic witch was meaner than a viper. "Ah, Norman, you're not as smart as you think. You've allowed her to escape."

"How would you know?" I leveled my icy gaze on her, smiling, but not with my eyes.

She looked out over Pennsylvania Ave. "The same way I keep taps on you." She laughed. "I watched the angel escape with your prize."

"Where is she now?" I sipped my bourbon, watching who exited which doors across the street.

"Underneath the oceans."

Carman moved behind me, siphoning a bit of my energy. "You've fed enough."

"How do you propose I deal with the Sarim prince?" Her corporal body solidified. "He'll need to be eliminated."

"Without an angel blade, the feat's practically impossible."

She snatched my whiskey tumbler and drank. "If the angel claims her, you'll need a removal spell."

I stepped inside, grabbed the decanter, poured myself another bourbon, and topped off Carman's glass. "What's your price?"

A sardonic smile curved her lips. I was morbidly curious about her devious ideas.

"If she's shifted, I don't need you, but I do want the angel."

"Why?"

"An exchange for the release of my three sons."

"How will we accomplish that?"

"When the silver wolf begins to experience her powers, she'll be weak. I will use her life force to pierce the thinning veil and break Odin's chains forever. Then you can carry on with your revenge. She'll be useless to her people once I locate the cauldron of wisdom she wears."

"Deal."

Carman's sharp nail tore a small gash in my palm, then her own. Our blood mingled, and a red thread wove itself around our wrists in a binding spell.

"Tell me your plans."

Carman settled into the chair as though she owned the place. "Grace's image will continue to appear in Cape Cod. The media will report Grace and you have secretly eloped. Won't the little wolf be surprised when she finds herself married?"

"Ahh! One way to keep the angel secret. Can't introduce a new love interest on your honeymoon." She grinned.

"Don't fret. You'll have your angel."

The irony suited my dark mood. I stepped away from her and turned to the living room, where Sheila played in front of the big screen. I was determined to exact retribution for my sister. The price for breaking the coven's laws was worth every sacrifice.

Carman's strength waned, her projection flickering before fading. She might become a problem later, but for now I needed her Seidr knowledge to complete my plan.

What did it matter if she sought power, so long as I had my vengeance? I chuckled and walked to the living room to play with Sheila. Once I stole the silver wolf's magic, I would decimate the shifters around the world.

Chapter Twenty-One

GRACE

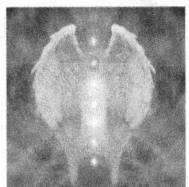

Two days passed since the trident marking. My feelings were so uncertain. I knew I was falling in love with Ananiel, but at the moment, we had so many roadblocks in our way. I reread his note to meet him in the dining hall, where Moira and Juna waited to join me for breakfast.

Refreshed and dressed in a tank top and workout pants, I entered.

With the sweetest of smiles, Moira embraced me. "I've got pineapple crumb cake on the table."

"I hope you zapped it with a dash of spirit and courage."

She leaned in close. "I've made a new batch of caramel bites to help with your anxiety."

"I will need them." Against the dining room wall, next to the steel double doors that lead to the kitchen, Jeffrey created a self-serve brunch with roast beef, lamb, and a variety of fanciful quiches. Roger and Dustin, along with the three Norn wolves, were accompanying me back to the White House to protect the shifters during the summit. Relieved to have the extra security, I could concentrate on getting my life in order.

I'd have to do a press release before the public learned the truth. Leslie, my best friend, was an investigative reporter and covered political news. Once anyone learned the truth, who knew if I'd even keep my presidency? I needed to return to work and reclaim control of my life.

"Hey, sis," Roger said, sitting next to me.

"What's the agenda?"

Sebastian, one of the Norn wolves, approached the table. "We've set up your new security squad. By evening they'll be in place. Vlad used mind control to reprogram the security staff into accepting their reassignment. It's crucial the humans don't detect the magical influence within the shifter council or the Secretary of Homeland Security."

Explaining the truth of my existence would be hard enough, but having the White House filled with supernaturals threatened the comfort level of mortals. My cabinet distrusted those who used magic or had special super strength. Laws prevented its use within the general population. Magical cities used cloaking spells to hide from the public. Most people feared the loss of control. Deep within my heart, I knew equality and acceptance depended upon fairness for every species.

A group of Nephilim women headed to the buffet table. Juna and Kai nodded in my direction.

Juna would be my right-hand security, taking on the leadership of the Secret Service.

I wanted to test out my new telekinesis and see the power's uses. Taking a concentrated breath, I visualized Juna's weapon and gently removed her knife from its sheath inside her leather boot.

As I pulled the knife from the sheath, Juna caught her blade and gave me a knowing smile as I manipulated the metals in the room. Shock registered, and the occupants turned in my direction as a stockpile of hidden odds and ends landed on our table. "New talent?" My brother asked, twisting a corner of his mouth into a grin at the variety of gadgets I'd uncovered.

"Great skill. I'm sure you've unnerved a few people this morning," Moira said as people retrieved their hardware and walked back to their tables.

"My body's thrumming with energy as if I don't release the power I'll explode." Turning to Moira, knowing she'd understand my dilemma.

"You need training. You're like a loaf of bread. With too much yeast and the bread blows and makes one colossal mess in the oven."

A surge of strange magic clutched at my belly, causing me to double over. On impulse, I reached for my locket. I grew dizzy and swooned.

Roger slid his arms around my waist and took me from the room. "Get Ananiel," he bellowed at Dustin before gazing at me. "You're pale."

Roger helped me to the couch in the community room and brought me a glass of water.

"I felt like a jolt of lightning zoomed through me when I touched Mom's locket."

Roger lowered his gaze and lifted the pendant from my throat. "The locket's part of the magic. Inside are the ancient spells of the wolves. The cauldron of knowledge."

Ananiel reached my side. "What happened?" He brushed his fingers through my hair and gazed down at my face.

"An energy power purge, I think."

I sat facing a panoramic view of a valley of wildflowers. The scene calmed me. "I feel better. So much magic surged through me after I touched the locket. My body short-circuited, overwhelmed from the intense energy soaring through my system."

"Moira will create a soothing potion to help shield your powers. We can't afford you the leisure of coming into your gifts. And I can't risk another unexpected wave of nausea. Next time, you might have no one around to help." Ananiel gave Roger a nod.

"What other changes do you expect to happen?" Frustration spilled out in a fiery sigh of pent-up emotions. The feelings were like a volcanic eruption ready to spew hot air.

"Can you breathe in the energy of another?"

"I haven't tried." I touched his arm and focused my thoughts. Green waves stormed through me, and the call of the wind whistled around me. As I began to siphon his energy into my own, the force field grew stronger before his shields blocked me from taking more.

"I thought so. When you do, you can harness another's talent."

"What?" I stammered and struggled to get off the couch.

"If you don't manage some shielding skills, the new magic will destroy your body."

"Holy fuck."

Moira and Juna came up beside me.

"Come on, Wolfie, we've got some work to do," Juna said.

Dustin entered the room with a cup of gobi tea. "Wolfie." He wrinkled his forehead at Juna.

The strange magic seemed like a cruel joke out of the Twilight Zone. One week ago, I was a normal woman with no special powers, and now I had the potential to take down the gods themselves. Let me slap myself and wake up from this crazy dream.

Poseidon stepped from the dining hall carrying his trident and looked powerful with his long white hair and beard. His massive size appeared dwarfed against the Nephilim cadets in their black suits and sunglasses. For a moment I felt like I was Will Smith in Men in Black paired with the straight-laced Tommy Lee Jones. Our goal: to cleanse the universe of scum.

Ananiel quirked his lip at me. "Men in Black!"

Apparently, he was reading my mind, a talent he'd seemed to polish since the claiming. What would happen once we became truly bonded? "That's what the cadets remind me of."

Gabriel and Zadkiel came out of the dining room and joined us in the community room. The room overflowed with people, and I felt embarrassed. Gabriel reached for my hand and pulled me to a standing position. "I like your sense of humor. We'll use it as our code when talking wolf business."

"I agree," Zadkiel said. "Now, go with Moira. She'll give you some teleporting potions and an arsenal of other useful items."

"In three days, Seth from the Aiden pack will arrive in D.C.. We'll ensure the nephilim cadets are prepared to protect the shifter council." Dustin gave me a peck on the cheek. "The cadets' muscular size will make them effective enforcers against the overzealous humans."

"I agree."

"Thanks for the use of your condo." Roger also kissed me.

Time was limited. I had to gain control before returning to DC. Soon, the alphas from across the United States would convene to meet with Congress regarding the final vote. Should the legislation fail, potential civil unrest between species for territory would be dangerous for us all? "Roger, please protect the nieces."

"I've sent the guardian Nephilim to watch over the family. They'll be safe." Roger rubbed his knuckles along my cheeks. "I'm proud of you, little sister; you're a lovable Wolfie."

Juna and Kai chuckled, and I knew I'd never be rid of the nickname now that my brothers found it amusing. I pinched his cheek. "This Wolfie can still kick your butt."

His gaze shone with love, and I melted into his embrace.

"Watch your back," Roger said, kissing my nose.

Dustin took me in his arms and snuggled into my neck.

I wrapped my arms around him and squeezed with every ounce of my strength. I'd forgotten how much I'd miss them both.

"Be careful. Assume everyone is an enemy."

"Pinky promise." I took his face into my palms. "Love you."

"Love you too, little sister."

They left the community center with Poseidon, Zadkiel, and Gabriel to join the Norn wolves. I turned back and followed Moira and Juna with a tightness in my chest. Now that I embraced my wolf heritage, the need to be with a pack grew strong inside of me.

Chapter Twenty-Two

GRACE

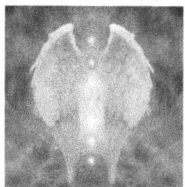

Later that afternoon, in the common room, Juna, Moira, Kai, and I practiced different magical scenarios in which I attempted to control the new powers. I had to proceed with caution.

Moira, a Seidr priestess, warned me the magical council wouldn't take kindly to a shifter using elemental fae magic. Many feared a magical war between supernaturals. The ley lines of power, if misused, threatened chaos and instability within the fragile balance of the human realms.

"Hot fudge cakes, you're powerful. You've broken through two of my protection wards," Moira said.

"I do not know what I'm doing." I laughed, completely intrigued with the concept of magic and the strange colors swirling around the room. Prior to shifting, I was lucky to boil water without help.

"Form a circle for this next exercise," Juna said. We sat arms link, but close enough to clasp hands.

I could hear deep breaths being taken around me.

"Focus your thoughts. Take one of the color streams and visualize the color. Let it become part of you and seep into your essence and grow inside your mind."

Moira's calming voice relaxed me, and I moved deeper into the experience.

My aunt would freak if she witnessed me imagining color schemes and their symbolic messages.

Soon, a light blue swath of light encompassed the room. I imagined lying on the grass, staring up at the clouds. A sea-blue calm wove around me, and it felt like Ananiel. That's what the color blue reminded me of —water, peace, and spirit.

"Blue. I like the color blue."

The girls chuckled.

Kai squeezed my hand. "Why blue?" she asked.

"The sea and Ananiel."

"Thought so." Kai nudged me.

"Come on Kai, don't tease our Wolfe, she's turning multiple shades of red."

I stood, stretching my sore muscles. My eye caught a crystal bowl sitting by the far wall. A light whistle sounded in my mind. I walked over and noticed a multiple mixture of small stones inside. I picked up a gold nugget with pieces of ruby inside. "What's this?"

"Zoisite. The stone harmonizes with the heart. Keep it close to you. The ruby will help keep you connected to what is true in your soul," Moira said, creating another mixture inside a wooden bowl.

"You mean Ananiel." Kai laughed.

She winked. "He is the next Sarim prince meant to reunite with his archeia."

I closed my hand around the small rock, wondering if we'd make it. I'd chosen him as my mate. He'd accepted, but a giant invisible barrier stood between us. The transition troubled him. I sensed it when he spoke with Seth and my brothers'. Being a celestial angel, he probably lacked understanding of the supernatural rules of pack society. "Did you know Uriel was the one for you when you first met?"

"We met at a basketball game on a mission to steal the infinity key from Luc. Our relationship started on unstable ground."

"What happened?" I sat on the couch next to her curious about her relationship with Uriel.

Juna and Kai sat on the floor.

"Brigit, my best friend and roommate, needed to go after a friend of ours who had taken a valuable book and disappeared into the demon realm. Brigit stole the key using one of my illusion potions."

"Ahh, if he's anything like Ananiel, I doubt it went over well with the angel," Juna said.

"It didn't. He can be one dominant pain in the biscuits."

"Why don't you say ass or fuck?" I asked.

Her eyes wide and round, she stared.

"Being a king's daughter, I was in the public, much like you are as president. I learned more entertaining ways to vent my frustrations."

"Got it. Your words make me laugh."

"My best friends say the same thing. Brigit likes to egg me on to see if I'll slip, but I never do. The habit's second nature."

"Making you have a slip of the tongue sounds like a challenge," Kai laughed.

I glanced away and chewed the corner of my lip. My own religious upbringing had strict rules regarding social behavior. But, like any orthodox girl, I had ways of ignoring the rules. I had a strange insight. I'd need that streak of rebellion in the next week. "I'm not sure I can help the supernatural community without revealing my identity."

"Humans and magical beings have lived in secret alongside each other for the last thirty years. Maybe it won't be as difficult as you believe," Moira said.

"Too many humans support the hunters, considering the shifters a step above a wild animal."

"That's why the civil rights amendment must pass," Juna chimed in. "Agreements need to be written to prevent distrust among the council leaders."

"I have faith you'll make the right decisions." Moira smiled and placed a hand on mine.

Grateful for her words of encouragement, I faced her. "You really believe the story of the kundalini dragon?"

"The curse is true."

"What if...?" I paused.

Kai and Juna moved in closer.

"The curse is a story passed down to all the nephilim. The Grigori watchers were sent to protect humanity after the great fall," Kai said.

"Ananiel's always made it his responsibility to guide and protect. I'm positive he's staying on the island because of his since of duty," Juna said.

"When did you know you loved Uriel more than just sexually?" I asked.

"Have you fallen in love with our stormy angel?" Moira clapped her hands with childlike glee.

I laughed and waved a hand, avoiding my actual feelings. "I want him more than I've ever wanted any man. I've marked him as my potential mate."

"But do you love him?" Kai tilted her head slightly, raising one brow.

Moisture filled my eyes, and I turned away, not capable of answering the question.

Moira wrapped her arms around me. "You'll find your way to each other, I promise."

"Thanks."

My locket grew warm in the cleavage of my breasts. I took the pendant in my hand while still holding the zoisite in my palm. The stone merged with my locket, creating a stunning ruby glow. "Fuck."

Kai and Juna moved in to get a closer look at my empty hand.

"Wow! Kai said. "I thought the Nephilim had special gifts, but none of us can merge objects.

"Another useful gift," Juna said.

Moira glanced at Kai, Juna and then turned her attention back to me. "Before returning to the White House, you need to understand the ether, which is the fifth element that connects all your elfin powers."

"Okay, what should we do?"

Using a piece of chalk, Moira drew two triangles on the floor representing the four elements of fire, water, air, and earth.

"First, take your place in the center of the ether triangle. We'll be using seidr magic, shamanism, to help you connect to your spiritual powers. This process is the only way to take control of the elemental power within your soul," Moira emphasized while I sat on the floor.

"Juna and Kai, each of you sit at the two points of the triangular shape, east and west." They sat cross-legged on either side.

Moira walked to the table and picked up a satchel. She opened the bag and pulled out a fossil shell. "Here are the ammonite fossils from the ocean to connect you to water." Moira said as she handed one to Juna and the other to Kai. "Set these between you and Grace."

"I'm placing green apophyllite encased in a dual pyramid to increase your abilities to perform rituals, sacraments, and open otherworld magical gates within the supernatural communities." Moira placed the gem in front of me. She reached in her satchel for another. "Hold this in your hand. The danburite spiritual enlightenment stone will keep you grounded during your etheric journey."

Kai kissed my cheek. "You ready?"

I hugged her close. "Yes, let's kick some ass."

"You're awesome."

"During the chant, I will call on the powers of Freya, the Nordic goddess of shamanic Seidr magic to help with the inward journey. Moira said the Norns would guide me, unlocking the ether element and revealing the akasha collective experiences of humankind.

My body trembled, feeling the vibrating power around me. Unexpectedly, I shifted into my wolf.

Juna ran her fingers through my thick fur, scratching behind my ears.

"Hello, Wolfie."

I nuzzled my nose under her hand. Our gazes met, and her calm presence centered the wolf's psyche.

"The silver wolf carries the knowledge, not Grace."

I barely heard Moira's soft murmur as she spoke to Kai.

A low growl emitted from deep in my throat. My ether spirit lifeline rose through the crown of the wolf's head.

The three chanted, "Ah-Gee-Awn, Tsah-Baw-Tsee-Yell."

I lost the sound of their words as my etheric body rose from my wolf.

In spirit, I glanced to the floor. Moira, Juna, and Kai slumped over their laps. A moment of panic seized my body, and I jerked on my etheric thread to take me back to my body. A soft gentle breeze whisked past me and I calmed feeling the guiding force of energy.

In my spiritual form, I roamed without the constraints of a physical body. I was in a large room connected to the dining hall, where we'd gathered for meals. Freedom of movement was like being in a dream. I wandered through the hall and saw Ananiel repairing furniture. His passion for the nephilims was clear in his care and love of the guild. I reached out and grazed his aura. His energy was angelic and beautiful, despite his gruff exterior.

I heard the voices of the Nordic Norns, and I drifted toward the enclosed gardens. When I'd arrived on Archipelago Island, claustrophobia filled me, now, I liked the depth of the ocean with the colorful sea life.

A faint image appeared like a hologram.

Urd in her corporeal form, smoothed a hand over my outer chakra. "Your truth lies within your core." She touched my heart chakra. "The choices you make will lighten or darken the path."

Verdandi lifted my hands into hers, palms open-faced. "Life or death burns within your hands."

"Honor the supernatural, the gods, and the humans with wisdom."

Their voices blended like a cacophony of violins.

The room spun around me. My spirit slipped back into the wolf. I stirred and lifted my snout. The others awoke and rose from their spots.

Juna and Kai sat on the couch. I shifted back into my body, and my fingers clenched my locket hanging in the cleft of my breast. "What happened?" I asked desperately for Moira to fill in my memory deficits.

"Your shaman journey appears fulfilled. I sense the increase in your spiritual powers." Moira smiled.

"I vaguely remember the Norn witches, but I don't recall what they said."

"You will, in time."

"Let's work with one of the four elements," Juna said.

I narrowed my gaze at the decorative candles sitting on the fireplace mantle. Slowly a flicker of light sparked and the candles lit. "Yes." I clapped my hands together.

"Fire element works," Kai said.

"Let's try for water. You up to messing around with Ananiel?" Moira asked.

"Why not?" I said, excited to see him.

"My kind of girl. Gotta keep those men of ours on their toes."

Moira's face was alive with mischief as she glanced from me to the dining room.

"What do you want me to do?"

"Imagine becoming a pool of water. See your skin liquify."

My skin tingled, and every molecule changed, much like when I shifted to wolf. Like a running stream, I moved underneath the door.

He sat leaning on his elbow, twisting a screw into place.

I stood before him and materialized naked.

He gazed with hot desire. "Water element."

"I can also light a candle."

"Did Moira show you how to taper down your energy and create shields to hide your magic?"

"Before we return to the surface, she wants her good friend, Katrina, to work with me. Apparently, she can channel the power of objects."

He chuckled. "When Uriel first met Moira, Katrina gained the use of his tattooed sword for a few weeks. Luc, Uriel's twin, still has Brigit's kiss burned into his flesh. Those two friends of Moira's know how to survive in the magical world."

Ananiel set the chair upright and left the tools on the seat. His hand slid down my spine, and his mouth found mine.

His kiss stole my breath, and I wrapped my arms around him, wanting to feel his body meld with mine.

"Tsk-tsk." I looked up over Ananiel's shoulder to see a mischievous twinkle lit in Moira's green eyes. "Thought you might need your clothes."

I gave her an evil glare.

"We've got work to do," she said without batting an eye. "Love can wait."

Juna stepped inside the dining room. "Incoming men."

I reached for my clothes and dressed. Ariel, Sophia, Uriel, Zadkiel, and a group of nephilim came inside ready for dinner as I finished pulling on my boots.

Jeffrey came through the kitchen and opened the doors to the buffet tables.

Projectors showed several holographic scenes of the White House throughout the dining room.

"After we eat, we've got work to accomplish before morning." Zadkiel said.

His brothers headed to the table, filling their plates like volcano pits, mixing who-knew-what together.

Uriel came over to stand next to his wife.

Ananiel took my elbow and steered me towards the grill where Jeffrey had a rare steak waiting.

My body craved the raw blood filled with iron. We selected our food and joined the others at our table.

"Juna will leave right after your talk and begin preparations for your arrival. After you are safely back in your office, you announce that, because of unfortunate circumstances, you will replace the current Secretary of Homeland Security. Before you arrive tomorrow, Juna will secure the nephilim in various jobs and positions," Zadkiel said.

"How do I identify who I can trust?" I slid my hand into Ananiel's, needing the comfort of his touch.

"I've cast an identifier spell on a pair of teardrop black tourmaline crystal earrings. Ananiel put them on your dressing table," Moira said.

Dinner finished, I met with Juna and prepared for my departure. My heart gave a little thump of relief at going home. I missed my best friend, Leslie. I needed to know what was happening at my office. Communication from my chief of staff had been nonexistent in the past week.

Ananiel curled his arms around me. "Are you ladies finished?"

Juna nodded and smiled. "We're ready for tomorrow, plans made. Get some rest."

Ananiel flashed us to his rooms.

When his hot mouth covered mine demanding his need, my breath hitched. A kaleidoscope of color swirled through us both, leaving my nerve endings sparking with energy.

Breaking his kiss, he framed my face in his large hands. "What is your safeword?"

"Stormy, like the man who's stealing my heart."

The rose of his cheeks revealed his vulnerability and weakness. My energy grabbed onto his, pulling him into me.

I threaded my fingers through his dark strands, pulling his neck to me. My wolf needed him to soothe the beast.

"Quit thinking, Wolfie. Open yourself to me."

A deep ache burned inside me, needing to tear down this emotional wall that felt as high as the Iron Curtain.

Chapter Twenty-Three

NORMAN

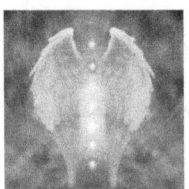

I sat at my desk contemplating my next moves. Grace would arrive in the next couple of days, if I'd calculated right. Her family, friends, and colleagues expected her back from Cape Cod tomorrow morning. With the upcoming Senate vote, I couldn't imagine her not making an appearance. Ten hours remained to set my scheme in motion.

I pressed the intercom button to my brother's room. "Meet me in my office." A few minutes later, a tap at the door, and David walked in.

"Let's talk."

"What's the game plan?" He poured himself a bourbon before settling into the leather chair opposite me.

"Jorge and I will move into the presidential living quarters and immediately announce to the staff my role as First Husband of the White House. No mix-ups can occur. Make sure Jorge uses glamour to maintain the illusion he's Grace."

"Jorge knows what to do. After you arrive, he will stay in the background until he is told that Grace's return is delayed."

"A press conference is scheduled to announce my recent marriage to the public. The media will eat it up."

"How will you keep her family and that journalist friend from barging in demanding to see her?"

"Her aunt and uncle won't risk exposure. They're Montana refuge members."

"Good. As chief of staff, I'll have her secretary intercept any unwanted guests. I'll spread the word that Grace is still celebrating our honeymoon."

"You'll buy a few hours, but security and her staff will expect her in a briefing."

"It's Sunday. We'll be fine as long as she returns Monday morning."

I leaned back and glanced at the FBI building through the window. "Any miscalculations and we're arrested before the magical communal."

David's concern showed. "Don't question me." I moved around the desk, grabbed his shirt, and hauled him out of his chair.

"Remove your hand from me." He stood his ground.

I unclenched my fist. "Grace knows I injected her. She won't accept our union quietly."

"Then give her little choice but to obey." David finished his bourbon and poured us each another.

"You're a cunning brute. What do you suggest?" I raised my glass.

"Make it clear. If she doesn't submit, you'll harm those she cherishes."

"Grace is no fool."

"No matter." He stepped onto the balcony. "The covens oppose the civil rights legislation—they fear it undermines supernaturals' authority in government." I joined him outside. "Next week, the shifters will be too busy to notice their ruin until it's too late. Once we eliminate the alpha leaders, the hunters will finish them."

"Grace's ties to the Aiden pack in Wyoming could work to our advantage. She won't risk her brother. And if she refuses, threaten to expose her as a wolf shifter. The public will see her as a traitor to the government."

"We walk a dangerous line."

"Don't forget what they did to our sister. Every wolf shifter deserves what happens."

Revenge drove me now. "Don't worry. I plan to make her suffer in ways she's never imagined."

"When she arrives, slip the gold wedding band on her finger. It's bound with a spell to block any magical powers she's gained." David pressed the ring into my hand; I pocketed it.

"Excellent. She'll pay for her betrayal. I'll harvest her power and taste it. I'll even let you have your turn when I'm done."

"You'll need an energy-drinker if you plan to steal her life force."

"I've struck a bargain with a powerful witch who owns the darkest black magic grimoire." I peered down at the crowd below.

"What about the angel?"

"I have other means to remove him. Watching his mate become mine will shatter his mind."

"Brother, do not betray me and claim her before I take my revenge." David faced me.

"You don't trust me?"

"Let's just say I believe you still have feelings for her."

My stomach knotted. "That was before she let another take what was mine."

"She was never yours alone." David's eyes narrowed.

"If you'd warded the trunk and stayed with her, we could've triggered her transition," I snarled.

"Watch your words," he growled back.

I ignored him and stared at the building across the street, imagining what was to come. "Once you're inside the White House, ward the second floor. Don't allow any supernaturals."

"I advise keeping Grace confined to her quarters as much as possible."

"I'll relish reacquainting myself with my wife."

Chapter Twenty-Four

GRACE

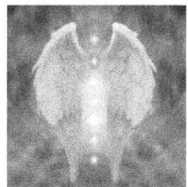

Red neon signs flashed in my mind. Warning! Go back—danger ahead. I had little choice but to ignore the vibes of destruction slamming into my mind. The insanity playing out before me caused me to question every one of my ethical beliefs.

Reports of my supposed marriage blared on every news station across the country. My body revolted at the idea. Why hadn't I seen who he was? What he was? The bite of regret twisted deep into my consciousness.

I'd gone to Harvard and excelled in politics, only to find myself in the middle of a deadly conflict between magical shifters and humans, all fighting for territorial rights. The pressure to unite the shifters weighed heavy on my soul. I'd denied the shifter side of my family in order to fit into society's expectations, but now I must lead the shifter population. Not only the wolves, but all shifters that survived on the outskirts of society.

As soon as I entered the White House courtyard, leading to the ground-floor kitchens of the residence building between the East and West wings. I had the strangest feeling that I'd walked into a labyrinth of mirrors like I'd once seen in a carnival. Illusions and traps were all around me. The magical wards tingled with a simple pattern of inter-crossing spells.

I chuckled. The mages who'd placed these incantations truly under-estimated my skills. Child's play. For now I'd leave them in place until I figured out what I was dealing with.

My A-V42 stiletto fighting knife strapped inside my boot was infused with Moira's paralyzing potions. I strapped a fanny pack of magical tools against my stomach and another pouch of potions around my thigh gave me reassurance, a backup strategy if everything else failed.

Using one of Moira's cloaking spells to deflect my presence, I entered the open courts on the North Portico and strolled down the basement hall away from the chocolate and flower rooms. I looked in the door of the Secret Service quarters to see the nephilim cadets had taken residency. I relaxed. Ready. I lowered my shoulders, and took a deep breath. I turned the corner to find Juna rounding the large stain-less-steel refrigerators. She wore a suitable suit.

Dropping the invisibility shield, my brow arched. "You clean up well, Ms. Juna Price."

"Come closer. You'll like what I have to show you." Her wrap around skirt detached easily from her body, same for her vest and blazer. Underneath, she wore black nylon stretch pants.

"I need the name of your seam-stress."

"I took the liberty and ordered you and Kai similar outfits."

"Appreciate it."

Juna embraced me and whispered in my ear, "The security of the residence is compromised."

"I can feel the wards." The effects of magic soared in the air, meaning Norman and his cronies were here.

"I've made arrangements for you to use the bedroom next to the solarium on the third floor of your residence. You'll be close to the gym in case you need to run and hide. Unfortunately, Norman's moved into your bedroom downstairs."

"Thanks for locating me a safe room. The wards and counter-wards charge the air. Can we have Moira deactivate some of this energy?" We continued through the basement hallway, past the chocolate and flower rooms. To the right was the Secret Services office.

"We don't wish to tip off the wizard of our own skills. Moira and Ananiel teleported inside to secure the environment against overzealous individuals invading your privacy. Norman, or his cronies, blocked Ananiel's signature from entering the residential rooms. He's furious and demands Yahweh return you to Archipelago Island."

"Typical alpha angel. Thinking I'm incapable of taking care of myself without his assistance."

"He's protective! You're his archeia."

"Not based on the media reports. How's he handling the press?"

"Like a tidal wave, hurricane, and volcano happening at the same time."

"That good?" I ran my hands along the front of my skirt preparing to face the firing squad of social media and the press. "Don't worry, I can deal with Norman. More than one mage signature is creating spells. At least two others." Only two weeks ago, I'd lived an ordinary human life. Now, every one of my senses was heightened and my eyes were opened to the multiverse.

"Kai will eavesdrop during her investigation. Be careful. Since Norman has claimed you as his wife, you'll have to play along for the present."

"We'll see." I'd misjudged him, believing him harmless. Sure, he resented my support of the shifters, but I figured his attitudes were like most Americans. I searched my memories for times when I'd ignored the red flags finding the illusionary comfort of his presence a joke on me.

"What are your thoughts?" Juna asked.

"First, I'd like to put my knife in his heart, for his treachery." A spot between my shoulder blades tingled with intense pressure.

"Stay calm. Now, let's take back the presidency."

My silk blouse and pencil skirt were completely unsuitable for fighting, but I had little choice. I was expected to give a national press conference within the hour. Apparently, my double returned with Norman the evening before, making sure to pose for the camera wearing a gold band on her left hand. I wanted to put my fingers around his slimy neck and squeeze. He'd used my darkest fears against me. The son of a bitch still thought he'd manipulate me. The game just changed, and I refused to lose.

The power of darkness swarmed in my blood and a burning fire filled my heart. I'd never hated anyone like Norm. I'd always known, or more like felt his cruel nature. His audacity to create this facade of a marriage ruined any chance of announcing Ananiel as my husband and mate.

"The mage masquerading as you slipped out last night. Norman is in the residential living room, awaiting your return.'"

"Keep him at bay until after I address the press, then I'll meet him in my study."

"We better get you to the West Wing without drawing too much attention." The cadets arrived. My very own 'men in black' formed lines on either side of me. I walked through the central hall, leaving the ground-floor residence for the press room in the West Wing. Looking at my watch, I had exactly fifteen minutes to figure out a plausible explanation that would satisfy the American people.

I reached for a caramel chew and popped it in my mouth. *Thank you, Moira.* My pulse pounded in my head. I had no idea how I would debunk the rumors of this false marriage.

Vice-President Forbes stood to my right. Directly to my left was Rochelle Dwain, secretary of the paranormal agency.

Lifting my chin, I hoped my posture portrayed the self-confidence I truly lacked.

I took my place. The first face I saw in the audience was Leslie. Her piercing cobalt eyes bored into my mine with an intense, angry expression. The granite set of her jaw left no doubt of her hurt. We'd been best friends our whole life and had always promised to be maid-of-honor in each other's wedding. How could I express this situation wasn't real but a hoax I couldn't prevent? Tears threatened to blind my vision. Her lips pursed and it was obvious her irritation threatened to override her good manners.

"Good afternoon," I addressed the group and pointed to a reporter standing to my left.

He asked the expected questions. "You've sent the shifter bill to the Senate floor for a vote. The American people believe you support the shifters over your own citizens. Would you state your reason for the legislation and why it's so important to you and your presidency?"

"The civil rights amendment will guarantee true equality. Every individual within our borders deserves an equal opportunity to reach their highest potential, no matter what species a person was born."

"Republican, Speaker of the House, Johnson states that each council tribe will be allowed to choose representatives and senate members based on the numbers in the districts they reside. Isn't it true they're already included in the census? So why should they have separate representation? Can you explain the special treatment?"

"Mr. Smith, the shifter communities lack services of any kind. They are denied basic rights, forced to live in crowded houses, poor neighborhoods, and most importantly, to live in fear for their lives. People hunt them for sport and justify their actions as protecting their communities from dangerous predators. Let me ask you, Mr. Smith—who is the victim when a hunter kills a packs of children in cold blood and without consequence? With this amendment, I am determined to ensure the right of every species to live without fear of death."

The crowd in the room grew silent.

In an attempt to calm my nerves, I inhaled a breath. Johnson, speaker of the House, was still a thorn in my side, but I knew how to deal with him. I wouldn't accept anything but an honest civil rights amendment.

"Madam President, during your trip to Cape Cod, you married your long-time fiancé. Some say you're pregnant. Is there any truth to the rumors?"

My mouth opened, and my tongue pushed slightly forward. I glanced toward Leslie for support. The whole idea of carrying Norman's child caused my skin to crawl in revulsion. I wanted this interview over. "I can assure you I'm not pregnant."

"Then why the secrecy of your nuptials?"

Microphones pushed toward me, and I stepped back, but there was no where to escape the onslaught.

"I've just arrived back at the White House after mourning the anniversary of my parent's deaths. The records, I assure you, will speak for themselves. I did not elope with Norman Hollered."

The crowd roared, with every reporter speaking at once.

Had I made life more difficult in denying Norman's claim? Rage surged through me. I knew Ananiel was somewhere in residence of the White House. His dominance filled the air. I wanted to say our safe word, but the interview was only the beginning. Until I learned the extent of the situation, I had to stay strong. Too much depended on making the right decisions.

Chapter Twenty-Five

ANANIEL

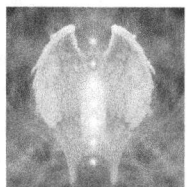

Inside Grace's bathroom shower of the presidential suites, I encountered a blocking spell. I wanted to check on her safety before I left to the Olympian pantheon. Fury raged through me, now the warlock was aware of my presence and my identity.

I flashed into the White House. Humans could not detect angel energy unless we wanted them to see our kind. This ability made it easy to fade into the shadows. Strong magical wards blocked my angelic powers throughout the second floor and into Grace's living room area. Irritated at my inability to disarm the spells, I slammed a fist against the force field in disgust.

Time ran short.

In ninety-six hours, a lunar eclipse would redden the night skies. The super blood wolf moon signified the end of the sexual frenzy and the start of the ceremonial bonding of mates. For the shifters to follow and trust the silver wolf, Grace and I needed to mate. Norman pretending to be her husband couldn't have happened at a worse time. She couldn't possibly complete the ritual while the American public thought she had married Norman.

The door opened, and Norman Hollered emerged with another

man, I assumed to be David by his side. The two men, wearing typical gray suits blended in with the other office staff.

A gold ring shimmered on Norman's left hand. Rage clawed through me and I wanted to rip the warlock to pieces for claiming my archeia as his. Until now, I didn't realize how much I cared for Grace. I followed the two men as they headed toward the East Wing.

Norman's stony expression revealed the darkness of his thoughts. A misty gray hatred surrounded both these men. Interesting. Hatred was a powerful motivator, and I'd guess the shifters were on the wrong side of these two mages. I'd find their Achilles' heels and exploit them before they hurt Grace. I'd be damned if these dark warlocks would destroy everything she wanted to accomplish for the good of all in the celestial pantheon.

Norman and David entered his office, and I followed. Norman's desk sat in the room, overlooking one of the many gardens. David sat across from him. I stayed shadowed in the corner, my strength growing weak from the warding spells. Clever. He'd warded the environment, preventing outsiders from using any powers not programmed into the spells. I scanned the room looking for personal clues, but found nothing except a photograph of a young woman. Pretty. She might be the bargaining chip I could use to keep Grace safe.

I stepped from the shadow.

Norman's face beamed with satisfaction. "We've been expecting you Sarim prince. You don't believe I was unaware of your presence?"

David stood, and a gleam shone in his gaze.

I turned to the warlock and attempted to read his mind. Blocked, which didn't surprise me.

"Take a seat, we've business to discuss.

I continued to stand, neither one sitting before the other.

"Both of you take a seat. Now." The restraint in his voice close to breaking.

David sat, I followed.

Ice burned in my soul. When this was over, I'd render them incapable of using magic against those too vulnerable to protect themselves from the elements. "What do you want with Grace?"

"She'll serve her purpose in a four days," Norman said.

I looked from Norman to David. "If the shifter treaty fails, a supernatural war is inevitable."

"Makes no difference to me. I have my own reasons for wanting to prevent the shifters from gaining a foothold inside the human communities," David said.

His venom was apparent in his tone.

"Gentlemen, I can promise you, you will fail." I rose and towered over Norman. My iron-muscled chest and six-five frame dwarfed his five-ten lean body. He'd break like a twig in the breeze. I turned toward the door, prepared to flash from the room, and find Grace.

His words stopped me. "We already have. As we speak, a reception celebrating my marriage to the President will occur in the Rose Garden. And I promise you, by the end of the week, she will submit to me during the wolf mating ceremony. This act will bind Grace's wolf until death."

The raw wound of my heart demanded I take action and eliminate the warlock before he caused more harm. "You're late. Grace has chosen and carries my mark. I've claimed her." My temper flared, and my wrath was upon him for even considering harm to my archeia. I knew, inside Grace's heart, she belonged to me and I to her.

Norman stood pointing his finger at my chest. "She's mine, you had no right to force her into a sexual frenzy with you." Norman seethed through clenched teeth. Anger boiled in his darkened eyes.

I'd let the mage believe he was in control. Once he slipped up, I was positive he'd provide me with an emotional button to use against him.

Her emotions danced in my heart and mind. The sigil thread connected our spirits. Never would she be alone. I regretted not standing with her as she faced down the reporters and challenged the American people, but she alone must lead.

Norman turned to David. "Go get my wife and bring her to my office, plans have changed."

"Are you ready?" David asked.

"Make sure her guard dog stays behind."

"If you cause her one moment of agony, I'll rip your throat out."

"Sit down. You're in my domain. Shut-up and listen to how we'll play this little game."

I drew in a hard breath. "You're a dead man."

The hate in his eyes burned deeper than the fires of hell. The very air around the man charged with dark energy.

Grace charged through the door like a whirlwind.

She stopped. Our gazes locked onto each other.

"What are you doing here?" Graces emerald eyes glistened and her heart hammered in her chest. Our sigil connection was even stronger since the claiming.

"Take a seat." Norman waved a hand in the direction of the chair.

"I'll stand." Her body stiffened.

Juna and David entered.

"Everything all right?" Juna asked.

She looked at me for conformation. At this point, I didn't know how much danger we might be in, especially since the wards prevented outside magick. But it was mid-morning and we couldn't draw attention to our purpose until after the passing of the legislation in Congress. This tied our hands and left us at the mercy of Norman for the next forty-eight hours.

Norman looked to Juna. "After lunch you'll be required at the reception, the President will be with me, and I'll escort her to lunch after our guest leaves."

I nodded to Juna and she backed out of the room. A wary concern etched across her brow, but we had to stick with the plan.

Grace moved closer to me until David pulled her toward the nearest leather chair. "Take a seat, Ms. Isaeva."

"David, you risk decapitation by touching me."

He backed off.

Norman moved from the protection of his desk and gripped Grace's wrist in his hand. "Unclench your fist," he told her.

I moved to reach for her but David held up his hand. "He won't hurt her."

Norman pinched the pressure point between her thumb and forefinger. Grace's fingers relaxed. He quickly slid the gold band around her finger before anyone could react. "Welcome home."

"What the fuck are you doing?" She yanked her hand out of his grasp.

"Taking back what's mine." Norman watched me, never taking his gaze from mine.

Grace's agony tore through me as she struggled to pull the ring from her finger.

A hot red flush swarmed her cheeks, and I knew something was amiss with her inner strength. Her gaze darted to me then back to Norman. "You've enchanted the ring."

"Just enough magic to encourage your compliance. And if that doesn't warrant your obedience. I'll eliminate one of your cousins." He brought her fingers to his mouth and kissed her hand.

I exploded with fiery rage and charged for Norman, but David sent out a bolt of energy knocking me backwards.

Grace jerked away "Leave my family out of your deceit. They know little of the magical or shifter worlds."

"Won't your cousins be surprised after they learn their golden-meal ticket is a shifter wolf? I can't wait to see their expressions when you're exposed to the American people."

A phantom figure materialized, looking like a ninja fighter except she wore a black layered skirt. The essence latched onto Grace and drew on her light.

"Stop her!" My voice boomed as I realized the witch stole life energy from other souls. A light-drinker. I hadn't seen one since the angelic council exterminated the witches for their horrific crimes. Grace's energy faded as the witch fed.

"She tastes good." Her physical essence became denser than Grace's skin grew pale, and she lost consciousness.

"Enough." I raged with blind fury and reached for her throat wrapping my hands around her neck and squeezed.

Her penetrating gaze never wavered while her breath pulled my angelic force from me.

I released my grip as my body crippled to the floor in agonizing pain.

"Secure him." David ordered.

The female handed him rope. "Tie him up with the antiquity rope I used to hold Freyr in Odin's prison. No god or angel can escape its iron grip." The witch's deep voice left no room for argument.

"Who are you?"

"I'm Carman." I recognized who she was and remembered the Norns prophecy that through Grace she'd escape her bondage from Odin. I hadn't wanted to believe it possible.

The seven antiquity metals of silver, gold, copper, lead, tin, and iron captured gods and angels. Determined to stay strong for Grace, I pushed away thoughts of thralldom, which is why most used the rope. I didn't plan on being anyone's slave.

"You don't want to miss what happens next."

Norman yanked me to my feet and pushed me into the chair to watch. His haunting tone chilled me like nails scratching down a chalkboard.

"Harm her in any way..."

"You'll watch everything I do, unable to help her in the least. I'm taking back what's mine." Norman lifted Grace into his arms and sat her on the desk.

Grace's head slumped forward. Her chin drooped against her shoulder.

"Wake her," Norman said, yanking up her head.

"Hand me a bottle of the restorative fluid out of the cooler behind Norman's desk," David said.

The witch walked over and brought the cooler to him. She reached inside and pulled out a plastic bottle of golden orange liquid, along with a syringe of a light blue substance, and gave them to David.

I struggled against the restraints.

"Relax, it won't be long before you'll be begging for death." A dark, wicked smile curved around her bright red lips.

"Bind her hands with the same silver cord, then make her drink the potion."

As she swallowed the liquid, tears formed on her cheeks.

The anguish ripped through my soul. How had we not been aware of their strength? The warlock's dark energy continued to feed the wards in the room.

Grace turned toward me. "Stormy," She whispered hoarsely.

Never in all my life had I experienced such helplessness. I swore each of them would suffer a celestial wrath worse than any torture in hell.

My heart bled for the pain in Grace's eyes. I'd sacrifice my soul to see her smile one more time.

Norman yanked her blouse down, revealing the trident on her right shoulder. "Remove it." He turned to the witch.

Carman leaned close to Grace and placed her mouth over hers. Then she injected the trident mark with the blue substance. A haunting laugh filled the empty space, and a coldness that turned the flesh to stone.

Grace's cries tore through me. I tried to move, but the cord tightened against my torso like cold steel.

The witch faded and disappeared as if someone had ripped her back through the otherworld doorway.

As if on cue, a grayish diamond light shimmered on the wall where a crystal portal opened. The long, flowing hair danced around her black dress. Strapped around her forearm was the Celtic cross of evil magic. The Greek Celtic druids were the darkest of the dark. Since the days of the great fae wars, the dark sidhe terrorized humans with their use of magic, separating the magical and humans. Carman, one of the evilest witches of the Greek pantheon, stepped through in her true physical form. In her hands, she carried a long, silver, triple-edged dagger. At the cross section of the blade is a three-pointed star, an angel blade. The one weapon that could kill angels, demons, and other supernatural beings. I kicked out my feet to escape her approach.

"I see you recognize the blade."

The dagger gleamed against her fingerless black-lace-gloves. She grinned when she sauntered toward me and placed one hand on my shoulders. She leaned in closer. Her mouth inches from mine, she pulled at my water elements.

"So full of tempestuous rage. The scent of the salty sea and Poseidon."

My angelic element of water pulled at her molecules, hoping to challenge her solidification. But she was whole and had escaped her prison. In my current predicament, I stood little chance of suppressing her power since she drank the light of the silver wolf, making her as strong as the gods. "Poseidon's wrath will see you destroyed, should you harm one of the nephilim."

"I have little interest in the half-breeds of angels or any argument with the Greek gods. My revenge is against Moira, the first of the kundalini archeia. With your death, the kundalini dragon can't rise. The dark lords will rule over the mortal realms throughout the pantheons."

The link between Grace and I resonated her pain.

Don't hurt him," she cried out.

Carman gave her a quick, piercing stare of hatred before devoting her attention to me.

David stood at the door and Norman entered another injection into Grace's shoulder.

"Poseidon always was a pain in the ass. Flooding the city of Athens because he lost the challenge to Athena. What weakness! But now I have bested his favored warrior, destroying the leader of the Grigori watchers."

"You condemn the mortal realm to a blood bath."

I spat in her face, determined to rile her anger.

The Celtic witch's mouth covered mine, and she feasted on my rage with her insatiable appetite for cruelty.

I twisted my head in disdain. "You bitch."

"Enough. Bring me the dagger," David said.

I slumped deeper into the chair.

She offered the blade to David.

He grasped the angel blade, placed it over the trident marking on Grace's shoulder and recited, "Libeashio Avulso." A fluid purple stream of fragments drew out of the angelic blade and into Grace's shoulder.

The pain rippled through my groin, the sacral chakra of the trident broken. My body spasmed. My chest burned, the pain tore at my soul, but I refused to lose our sigil connection.

"His spirit is strong, he won't surrender the connection," David said.

"He will after he witnesses the removal of his mark." Norman took out a third syringe and injected Grace's left shoulder. Acidic bubbles burned along the trident. "Extieuous Pestiate, expunge the marking from the wolf."

As the trident erased from Grace's shoulder, she writhed on the desk.

I reached through the sigil bond and sent her my love. *"I'm sorry."*

Her face turned to me and somehow, she got to her feet. Grace tried to slam her body into Carman's but missed and collapsed on the floor.

"Feisty female," Carman said.

"The nephilim have called in Freya and Moira. The Seidr witches have already broken through our barriers. You best accomplish what you want before your time runs out," David snarled, looking down at me, weak and unable to protect Grace.

Nuriel's, angelic charm challenged the mage's removal skills, leaving my body raging with pain.

The warlock lowered the knife. "Without the fire sword, I can't remove the sigil signature."

"Then leave him in Niflheim to rot in the primordial darkness of the lost souls." Norman picked up Grace from the floor, reached into the ice chest and pulled out a teleporting ball. He disappeared in a swirling pool of pulsing light.

"Clean up the mess." David pulled another teleporting ball from the chest and teleported, too, leaving me with Carman.

"The gods' gift of opening the portal has served me well." She tossed my body inside the icy coldness of Niflheim and closed the portal.

Chapter Twenty-Six

GRACE

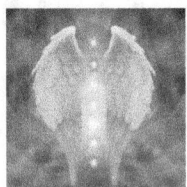

My eye slowly opened to tan colored walls with paisley flowers. Raw pain burned my shoulder. My body felt as if it had been used to scrub the floor. My gaze took in the familiar surroundings of the presidential residence. I slept in my own bed with no recall of how I'd gotten here.

Leslie sat beside me, wiping my face with a damp cloth.

Nausea hit. I winced in pain and doubted I'd survive any more torture. Tears streamed down my cheeks at the prospect of Ananiel forever trapped in the world of the dead. How could I explain to Leslie and make her understand that Norman was a killer? Betrayal fired through my blood. The man I'd shared my life with tried to kill me, but he failed.

"How are you feeling?" Concern reflected in her eyes.

"How long have I slept?" I struggled to rise. A piercing jab stabbed through my shoulder blade. I reached to touch the scar, but it had healed like it never existed. A new sense of fury filled my soul, and I forced myself from the bed. I wavered on my feet, but no way would Norman get away with destroying the man I loved.

"Ten hours." Leslie took my arm and helped me to the bathroom. "What's up with the new hair streaks?"

"What?" The question seemed to come out of thin air. I'd forgotten the change in my appearance. "I weaved my hair in Cape Cod."

"Cute look."

The bitter agony that welled inside me threatened to break my resolve. "Thanks." I turned the water on in the sink and braced my hands against the mirror. The bags under my eyes didn't bode well for winning any beauty contest. Running my fingers through the ragged strands, I attempted to smooth down the stray pieces of hair. A buzzing sound came from the shower. The chute Ananiel had told me about. The way back to Archipelago Island if I was in danger. Ananiel wasn't there, but I could send a message to Ariel and Sophia. I reached into my cosmetic drawer and took out a black eyeliner pencil. On a hand towel, I wrote, *Ananiel in danger! In Niflheim. Hurt!* I dropped the towel inside the chute and hoped that Jeffrey would find it.

I whispered a silent prayer, hoping my message fell into the right hands. I wanted to leave and get away from Norman, but if I did what would become of the shifter legislation, they depended on me.

Leslie waited on the bed. "Do you remember what happened? Norman said you collapsed outside in the Rose Garden."

A wave of apprehension washed over me. He'd told lies to my family, my friends, and my associates. Norman's torture still lived inside me. Memories of being buried alive couldn't compare to the terror I felt when he stripped me of Ananiel's mark. I wanted to tell Leslie the truth, but she'd never believe I'd been taken against my will. "Where's Norman?"

"He mentioned an early morning run."

"Where's my Security chief I need to speak with her." Who had changed my clothes?

"I'm sure she's just waking up." She looked at her smart watch. "It's 4:00 in the morning."

"What are you doing here?" I looked through the drawers and the writing desk in hopes of finding my knife. I was uncertain if Leslie spoke the truth. The idea Norman allowed her to stay seemed fishy.

"After the press conference, you disappeared and I wanted to talk to you. I refused to leave." She backed away as I scrambled around the room.

"Norman let you stay?"

"Your security woman, Juna, convinced him that if he wouldn't call an ambulance when you fainted, someone should be with you if you needed help."

I dropped to the bed, discouraged Norman found my weapon and potions.

"Suppose that makes sense."

"Your aunt and uncle will be here tonight. Norman's arranged a family gathering to celebrate your marriage."

"I need to tell you something." I reached for her arm. "Norman and I aren't married."

Leslie lifted my left hand. "You look married to me."

I pulled at the ring and still couldn't remove it from my finger. The magic woven in the metal tampered with my wolf's ability to shift. I couldn't even communicate or feel her inside of me. If he prevented the silver wolf from taking a leadership role with the shifters, then it meant the Aiden pack and the other shifters faced Congress alone. "I need to tell you a secret. A secret I've kept hidden since my parents' deaths."

Leslie took a long, slow breath and gave me a strange roll of her eyes. "All right."

The hurt tone in her voice made me wonder if Leslie still harbored feelings about not being my maid of honor at a wedding that never existed.

"Not here. Trust me. Everything will make perfect sense."

"Where?" She stood, offered me her hand, and gave me an encouraging smile.

Her trust soothed my aching soul. I needed my childhood friend on my side if I was to survive the next few days.

"Juna secured me the southwest bedroom on the third floor. The room closest to the athletic center. If we run into anyone, they'll think I'm completing my morning workout."

Leslie's brows crinkled, but she'd understand once she learned the truth.

I slipped on a pair of jeans and a sweat-shirt. I fumbled around one more time in hopes of finding my knife. I could only hope Juna took it from my person before Norman found it. "Hurry, we don't have time.

If Norman learns I'm awake, I'm positive he won't let me out of his sight."

We slipped out of the suite and took the elevator to the central hall. Frustrated at my inability to use my new powers of observation, I jumped at every creaking movement along the hallway. We came to the largest bedroom facing the promenade. I placed both palms on the door and listened for a low humming energy signaling Moira's spell work, but my magick was blocked.

We entered the room, and I released the tension in my shoulders. On the dressing table lay my fanny-pack of potions, along with my A-V42 stiletto. I immediately attached my blade to my thigh, took out a teleporting ball, and put the potion in my pocket.

"You're really starting to freak me out. What's all this and what are you involved in?"

"Trust me."

The thought of Ananiel sickened me, and I pushed back the tears threatening to spill from my eyes. Ananiel still lived. I felt the strength of our sigil connection. Pulling deep inside my core, I tried to reach for the link, but the bond was weak.

"What's up?" Her eyes narrowed.

I felt her take an emotional step back. Leslie knew of my skill with knives. In fact, she'd trained with me and her own skill matched mine. How did I start? "On our way home after Shelby's graduation, Norm injected me with a paralyzing serum."

"You're saying Norman tried to paralyze you?" Her eyelids widen in complete disbelief.

"That's what I believed at first, but now I think he wants to humiliate and discredit me in front of the American people."

"What you're saying doesn't make one bit of logical sense. Why would he desire to harm any part of you?"

I reached for my locket with my left hand and pushed my finger over the zoisite stone embedded within. What if I could cause the gold in the ring to merge? I pulled my hand away. The ring still clung to my finger, but tingles of energy threaded through my fingers. I shuddered with possibility, the gems and the stones might help me break the spell bound within the gold metal.

A knot of tension settled in my stomach as I faced my best friend's possible rejection of who I was. I needed one of Moira's caramels to help me focus my thoughts.

"I'm a wolf. So are Roger and Dustin."

Her eyes widened, she opened her mouth to speak, but no words emerged. With a heavy sigh, she walked to the large window, and looked out over the promenade. "A shifter. Now I get why this legislation's so important to you."

The soft timbre of her voice soothed me into believing in her acceptance of who I was.

"My brothers belong to the Yellowstone pack in Wyoming."

Leslie gave a dry laugh. "That's why Roger said we couldn't marry. Your brother must be afraid, if I learned the truth, I wouldn't want him."

I couldn't tell her the real reason. Roger never believed she'd fit in as a shifter's mate. Even though shifters weren't immortal, their healing abilities allowed them to live double the span of a human. "There's more."

Her brows knitted together and she frowned. She turned to face me. "Spill it."

"Apparently, I'm meant to unite the wolf clans. If the American people refuse to create a treaty of equality, the shifter council intends to start a territorial war for land. They want the destruction of their homes and families to stop." A tightness gripped my chest for the misery inflicted on innocent people.

"I know. The massacre at the schoolhouse worked up a lot of people. The shifter council's demanding execution for the unwarranted murder of their children. One of the staff reporters is following the story."

"No one has the right to kill and desecrate the packs. The hunters must be brought to justice." Tears burned my eyes and I pushed down the lump threatening my ability to speak.

"Is there more?"

Unable to sit, I opened the mini refrigerator and pulled out two waters. "Here."

She took a swallow.

I needed to regain a semblance of composure. "That's not the worst of the story, but I need you to trust and help me.

A sea of expressions crossed Leslie's face. "What do you want me to do?"

"Contact Roger. The White House records all phone calls. He's staying at my condo in Georgetown. Tell him Norman's using powerful magic with the help of a witch who escaped Odin's prison."

Leslie blanched and mouthed, "Odin's prison."

"Have him warn the council. Tell Juna and the 'Men in Black' I need the gemstones. She'll understand.

"Men in Black?" Her incredulous look said I must be out of my mind. All I could do was shrug my shoulders.

"I'll explain later; just tell Roger. We're out of time, and if Norman knows you are aware of who he is, I fear for your life." A part of me felt guilty for involving Leslie, but as an investigative reporter, she was the perfect ally to help me in my plan to expose him and the hunters before they hurt any more people. Rubbing the back of my neck, I hoped I had made the right decision.

"Great!" She cleared her throat with uncharacteristic nervousness. "You can't stay here." She reached for my hand.

"Trust me. I have a plan. I'm president, if I leave, he wins. I look like a coward. The legislation comes first, then I'll expose them for who they are."

"Sounds dangerous." She wrapped her arms around me. "I got your back."

"Follow me." We left the room and headed down the hall to the gym.

I put my forefinger over my lips. I'd taken a risk in confiding in Leslie, I had to believe Juna debugged my safe room. Inside the gym, I picked up a phone and punched the number into Juna's direct line, knowing this would immediately alert Norman or David.

My routine must be believable if I had any chance of fooling the warlocks. I twirled the gold band on my finger, ecstatic that my mother's locket had given me the clue to breaking the magic binding me to the ring. Closing my eyes, a surge of gratitude wash over me knowing I had the element of surprise.

Chapter Twenty-Seven

ANANIEL

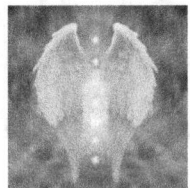

I awoke to a stark blue sky. My body lay near the portal bridge entering Niflheim. The last thing I expected was a crystal-clear day in the realm of the dead. Birds chirped overhead, bringing the soul of the living to the underworld. In the cold isolation of Niflheim, I expected carrion scavengers instead of the bluejays swirling above me.

"Welcome to my realm, archangel." The Nordic goddess of the dead extended her right hand and pulled me to my feet.

I gazed into the most compelling sapphire eyes. Her glossy lips brightened half her face while the other sagged in nothingness. The left side of her body was an icy, pearly shadow of her right. A skeletal reflection of the beauty she once was before Odin threw her out of Asgard. She turned her attractive side to the bright morning light, scrutinizing me.

"Hel?"

"And you, archangel, have trespassed into my realm."

"Not by choice."

"Your flesh is warm, and blood flows through your veins. You still live."

I grasped my ribs bound in antiquity metal rope meant to bind gods and angels from using their powers or used to hold one in captivity. "I find myself in a troublesome situation."

Her fingers traced the path of the binding rope that prevented me from returning to my realm. "Carman did this. Odin's prisoner has used her own rope against you."

"Can you remove them? Or do we need to locate Odin?"

Her head whipped around to reveal the hollow flesh of her body. "Odin has little to do with our realm except to send warriors unworthy of his glorious army."

As Hel's mood darkened, gray clouds huddled overhead. Apparently, the environment of Hel's realm reacted to her internal feelings. "Ruler of the great realm of Niflheim, the realm of the dead, I beseech your assistance in breaking these bonds that have entrapped me."

"In time—great archangel, first you will dine with me and Baldur tonight. He'll enjoy meeting the son of Yahweh of the celestial pantheon." Her rich voice flooded over her like warm honey.

I grasped the sardonic meaning of her words.

Yahweh expected the Grigori guardian angels to protect the mortals while he and Diablo continued with their wager for rulership over humanity. When he'd banished the goddess of death to live in Niflheim, Odin caused her to live out her life forever half alive and half dying amongst the dead.

"I'm honored to join the festivities in the great hall of Helheim." We left the gate along the river and continued through level one of Niflheim. Each step caused the metals of the rope to pierce deeper into my skin, leaving me weaker the deeper we maneuvered into the land of the dead.

Odin finds Carman's escape entertaining. He didn't expect the Celtic witch to manipulate Enki's gift to the silver wolf."

The unexpected assault left me furious at Odin for allowing one so evil to escape. "The witch deserves death," I hissed.

"Living in Niflheim and wandering the nine rings, Carman has gained alliance with those whose vengeance fills her heart. Her sons traverse Midgard, the realm of mortals much like your United States. The three offspring have mastered the skill of necromancy since being raised in the land of the dead. Beware, her armies grow large in preparation for the rise of the dark realm."

"You are ruler of the nine levels of Niflheim. Stop her before she destroys Moira."

"Aah, the baker. Delightful young warrior. I helped her and Uriel in their quest."

"Carman is out to kill my sister-in-law and prevent the rising of the kundalini." I stopped and lowered my pride to plead with Hel. "Carman can-not be allowed to roam the other pantheons. She's dangerous."

"Are you curious how she came to give birth to four children?"

The thought crossed my mind. "Moira mentioned her father being trapped."

"Carman captured Freyr in his search for Gerdr, his wife. She bound him and kept him captive until he impregnated her with quadruplets. She loved him, in her sadistic way."

"I'm sure she did." We continued walking through the first ring. Spirit shadows lingered, but not too close.

"The Celtic witch covets power, and Freyr promised to take her to Alfheim as his queen if she released the antiquity rope. She believes him. But he escaped with his daughter, leaving Carman tied to their mating bed."

My unrestrained laughter at Freyr's treachery filled the moment with a conceivable plan of escape.

Hel hooked her hand in the crook of my elbow. "Baldur awaits my return."

The sun illuminated the sky, and a valley of morning sun flowers swayed in the wild prairie fields. Not what I expected, but, like Hades, there were levels of death. I needed her and Odin's help.

A dark, foreboding element came through the gray hovering beyond Hel's hall. Three men on horses leaped over a rapidly flowing river and disappeared into the ether.

"Those are Carman's sons. They ride with the dark elfin ruler, Hagmer, in search of a way to cross the otherworld and enter your pantheon."

"Without the sacred key, no individual can traverse the realms." I carried my hatred of death and beyond. Soon, his wrath would be upon his enemies.

"Except ... immortal gods play by their own set of rules." Hel turned toward a second portal, leaving Niflheim.

"You believe Diablo helped Carman escape?" I didn't expect her to reveal the truth.

"The locket holds the knowledge to unlock the doors of every pantheon. If taken, it becomes a powerful weapon."

"Enki's gift to open a portal was Diablo's means to prevent the rise of the kundalini?" The scheme unfolded in my mind.

"You catch on quickly."

As tidbits returned to my memory, the Norns' warning buzzed like bees in my consciousness. Skuld had spoken to Moira, warning of her mother's escape.

"Will you help me return to the celestial realm? I am not dead and don't belong here."

We approached Hel's palace, where I expected sorrow, but within her dwelling was a grand dining hall. On the walls, sconces of light brightened the room. On a large oaken table sat a grand feast of charcoal-grilled reindeer with roasted leeks and berry cakes.

Baldur sat at the head of the table, and several of Odin's finest warriors were along the benches. Hel sat across from Baldur.

I took the seat to her left, struggling with the ropes binding my chest. With my arms free, I wiped the beads of moisture from my forehead and tried not to concentrate on the confinement of the ropes. "You honor me with a fine feast."

"Refresh your body and regain your strength." Baldur passed me a giant slab of meat.

A serving wench poured mead into Baldur's mug and my own.

"*Takk.*" Using the Nordic language for thanks, I raised the mead in honor and drank.

"You are a respectful man. And for that, I offer you these." She handed me two loaves of cake. "Use one loaf as payment, and Garmr will let you pass without harm. The land of the living is over the bridge close to where you arrived. Garmr guards my home and prevents the dead from crossing into the realms of the living. You are free to leave."

"Unbind me and I can flash back to my realm."

"I lack the power to remove the seven metals of antiquity." She ran her finger along the rope. "I will ease your discomfort until you leave here."

"Your generosity is appreciated, but why?"

"I want you to succeed—Moira, the mother of the kundalini, is the root. Grace is the sacral. If the pantheons lose their way and the balance is unhinged, our universe will die."

We finished our meal in silence.

Then Baldur walked me out through the vast emptiness of space, with stark grayness in place of blue sky. A shadow of mist covered the land, which would make my journey across the bridge a precarious adventure.

"Siller reiser." Baldur faded into the fog, leaving me alone.

"Safe travels," I repeated his words sensing the cries of the dead emerging from the rapid rage of the river below.

Chapter Twenty-Eight

ANANIEL

Lightning lashed the sky with jagged streaks of gold, illuminating the path along the river of Niflheim. The reviving tune of the water coaxed my body to relax from the throbbing pain. As I approached the portal into the living world, the ropes cut deeper into my chest. More storm clouds merged, and the air was alive with electricity along the river of death. The savage rage of thunder announced the recently dead. Slowly, I reached the crossroads between life and death.

Garmr, the magnificent wolf, snarled and paced back and forth. His chains rattled against the wooden planks. And I took one of the 'Hel-cakes' the queen of Niflheim gave me as payment.

He growled in acknowledgment and backed into the dark regions, allowing me to pass. I left one loaf of cake halfway across, and I'd leave the other at the end of the bridge.

"Ananiel, watch out." Gavin, my security man, near-frantic tone alerted me to the three riders coming toward me from the outer borders of the realm. Hel warned me that Carman's son traversed the realms and searched for a way to leave the Nordic pantheon. Unable to flash or use any of my supernatural abilities, I, the angel of wrath, dug deep into the rage stored inside the riders' souls. My strength grew darker. I drew on the destructive force of evil I pulled from the necromancers. I used their own fear of judgement against them. While the three men battled their own demons, I dashed through the portal into the living world.

Never in all my life was I so excited to see chute six.

Gavin reached me and tugged me to the open tubular and back to the docks on Archipelago Island.

Ariel touched my arm but instantly backed away. "Warlock magic."

Fear was clearly visible on his blanched face.

My heart hammered as the salty sea air reached my skin. Pain surged through me, and I gasped as my breath caught in my throat. "They intended for him to die a slow, agonizing death if he escaped and returned to the sea." Ariel's colorless face scared even me.

"We've got to remove the spell." Gavin gritted his teeth at the swelling blisters forming along the edges of the rope. He reached to pull at the rope.

An electrical shock jolted through my body.

Gavin jerked his hand away.

"We'll need Moira." Ariel's white knuckles fisted at his side. "I'll be back." Ariel left through chute one, leading to the surface of the human realm.

I stumbled onto one knee. With every stabbing pain, I visualized how I'd target Norman and David's most painful regret and make sure they whimpered with horror when I finished twisting every fiber of their bodies. The salty sea air continued to cause the oxidation of the metals within the rope. The constant jabs felt like Diablo's two-pronged fork electrocuting my flesh.

Gavin hooked his shoulder underneath my arm and walked me to the infirmary. The cadets continued to patrol the chutes, marching in nervous synchronicity. Had none of the Nephilim or the Grigori watchers seen me weak.

I tried to flash, but I couldn't.

The healers rushed from the healing center, taking me from Gavin's arms.

On the gurney, sweat beaded on my forehead as someone wiped my face with the cold cloth. "Grace." Was Grace here?"

I slipped into the depths of my mind, lost in fevered dreams. Dreams where I was chained, unable to escape their torture. Another sharp jolt sizzled along the length of my leg. "Father," I screamed, on the verge of insanity. "Help me."

A hand grasped mine and attempted to cool my flesh. "Grace." I mumbled, "help me."

A voice bellowed over the crowd, "These spells around the rope of antiquity come from the darkest of fires: black, red, and blue. Blue, the hottest of flames, are meant to kill the angels. Try using holy water from Kumuria's healing pools."

Samael, the prince of demons, his words echoed in my mind. *"Norman and Carman mean to kill you if you find a way to escape captivity."*

As the healers laid wet towels across my torso. My stomach pitched a fit and roared in protest as the warlocks poison rippled through my flesh, leaving blisters of unbearable pain. I pulled on the sigil connection to my archiea, Grace's love would help me survive.

Moira and Uriel burst through the door.

My vision faded in and out as their words blended as one. Something about Samael. Samael's allegiance to both Diablo and Yahweh.

"Strap him down," someone shouted.

A choir of angels flooded my room with angelic vibrational music. The words played continuously, *dying*. Only in the true death did the choir sing. They were bringing me to Tartarus. I can't leave Grace.

Images of magic swarmed through levels of darkness filling my heart. The light was fading.

"Holy Father." I lifted my body from the table. "Why have you forsaken me?" I grasped onto a man who resembled my father. Was he here?

No! My father hated me, considered me the seed of Diablo because I protected our hybrid children. Without the Nephilim, his precious humans would never have survived. The mortals fumbled around without guidance, without powers, and without knowledge. The Grigori angels did as Father requested, and he abandoned them without cause.

"What right did you have to sacrifice your angels over helpless mortals who still lack the powers of your original children?"

Someone laid another cool cloth across my face. A thrumming of choir chants surrounded me.

"Where is his archeia?" a woman with the sweetest lyrical voice.

I reached for him. "Uriel, help me." My hand fell away, and a tidal wave pulled me under. I scrambled to rise to the surface, but I couldn't breathe. What? The water filled me with peace and contentment, a perfect place to die.

But Poseidon continued to jab his trident into my back. "Decamp. Defect. Desert."

His words jumbled in my mind. "Who should I leave behind?"

His voice faded into nothingness. One by one, the others drifted into a foggy abyss. The choir of angels hovered over me, and my father prepared to take me home to Kumuria. I grasped for my lifeline to Grace; the sigil faded. I was losing her.

"Come, my son, you have accomplished all you can."

"The kundalini dragon will wither away into nothingness." Anguish filled the woman's tone.

"Mom." Gentle hands brushed my dried lips.

"I love you, my son."

"Mom." I reached for the feminine voice I hadn't heard in so many years. Not since the day my mother left my father.

I felt my arms drag over rigid edges. My body dehydrated, destroyed, and demolished me.

Diablo stood at the portal of the otherworld gateway.

My eyelids drooped closed. I wanted him to take my soul and end the madness invading me.

Without preamble, someone yanked the heavy metal off my chest.

Too late. My power was completely gone. Taken, I succumbed to the darkness in relief. "I'm sorry, my archeia, my love. Forgive me."

I wanted the true death, ashes to ashes, and never to return. The unbearable loss of my archeia for a second time. Being a failure, I, the angel of wrath, destroyed the universe. Soon, the dark would prevail, and Diablo would seize control over the celestial humans.

A breeze of cool air touched my torn flesh. As a pleasant sensation enveloped me, I sighed with relief, like being dropped into a pool of strawberry ice cream. I hadn't thought of strawberry ice cream since I was a little boy chasing Luc. Uriel and Luc were already teenagers when I was born. They enjoyed riling my temper.

As a child, I became enraged when confined too long in one space. I required the open seas, and the wind blowing in my face. Water splattered across me, and I welcomed the relief of returning home.

The stormy ocean called to my soul as Azrael, the angel of death, stood on the swelling waves of the raging seas. He held out his hand. "Come."

I touched Azrael's fingers, letting him take my soul. My spirit embraced the sea as regret of my failure filled my aching heart, knowing I'd caused the true death of my brothers and our archeia.

* * * *

Moira pulled back from the stifling crowd. The healing center was full of celestial choir angels hovering over the Sarim prince lying on his deathbed. The ancient Seidr wards comprised a unique complex of spells that few witches understood. Their potential to control the gods prevented the knowledge from being widely known. Apparently, the warlocks added their own weave to ensure his death should salty water touch the ropes.

If only she had the grimoire of magical spells. But Moira had left the third book in Niflheim when she'd escaped with her life. Leaving the ancient text behind held little consequence. Until now. Moira understood her mother's motives clearly, and her stomach flipped, making her shrink with guilt. The responsibility for Ananiel's dilemma rested on her shoulders. She'd known Carman's intent to escape Odin's prison.

Uriel slipped an arm around her waist. "Guilt traps you in hell. We knew the challenge. This is Ananiel's. Trust he'll make the right choices and believe in his archeia's love."

She lifted her face to his and accepted his gentle kiss. "Thanks."

"Anytime, buttercups."

His smile made her spirits soar with shameless delight and gave her the confidence to help Ananiel survive his ordeal.

None of the Sarim princes, nor their archeia mates, were out of danger from the necromancers and their dark energy until the last prince completed the kundalini. Last year, Moira and Uriel were the first Sarim pair to retrieve the red jasper from the magical grimoire.

Samael's golden wings covered Ananiel, protecting him from further evil penetrating his weakened body. "You must create the circle of seven to bring his spirit back." The warlock infused a separation spell on the chance we freed him from the ropes."

"Fudge cakes, this can't be happening." Moira said. "I can't seem to undo the ward. Each sigil symbol pairs with another. How is he doing this?"

"I can only assume the warlock is using telepathy to counteract every one of your healing weaves."

"Why?" Moira asked.

"Grace. The warlock has separated Ananiel's auric field from his physical body to ensure he doesn't return to the human realm. Ananiel's drifting in the ether—not dead, not living."

"Where does he go to reconnect when he needs to find solace?" Samael asked Uriel.

"He's a special spot on the far side of the island," Uriel said.

"That's where he and Grace accepted each other as mates," Sophia chimed in as she entered the healing room with fresh towels.

"And how would you know this bit of information?" Uriel asked.

"I know everything that takes place at the guild, it's my job."

Samael lifted Ananiel from the bed and turned to Moira. "I have an idea. We'll take him to the estuary where he and Grace accepted each other as mates. We've got to force him to return to his body."

Samael teleported with Ananiel.

Uriel wrapped Moira in his arms and teleported them to the small hidden cove on the isolated side of the island.

Vines of hedge maple over-lapped the soft ground, causing her to stumble onto her hands. "Don't laugh."

"Never." Uriel pushed her backside, forcing her to crawl inside the space.

The moon's mysterious light shone into the cozy enclosure. She stared upward, drawing in a shaky breath. They had two days before the blood moon filled the night sky. Would Grace and Ananiel fulfill their destiny? Or would the Sarim princes all face the true death?

"Fudge sticks," she hissed, wiping at the unwanted tears sliding down her cheeks. Pulling her knife from the sheath in her boot, Moira drew a square/triangle in the center of the clearing.

"The first of the seven metals of antiquity is gold," Uriel said.

Moira carved a circle with a focal center point inside.

Samael sprinkled elements of gold. "Done."

"Second is silver."

She drew a sliver of a quarter moon, and Samael added silver. They continued carving the ritual until it represented all seven elements.

In desperation, Moira looked into Uriel's eyes. She crossed her fingers for success.

Uriel's hand wiped at her tears. "You can do this. Take back what the warlock has stolen and return it to Ananiel."

Samael's fingers intertwined with Moira's, and he opened a one-way portal into a lavish apartment facing the FBI building along Ninth Street.

The stainless-steel kitchen had whitewashed walls, typical of the modern, angular condos. Moira absolutely hated the style, preferring more color and a touch of creativity in her home.

The warlock wore a gray Armani suit, his short blond hair slicked back. He leaned his elbows on the rail of a balcony.

They'd have to wait until he entered through the French doors of his office.

Samael interrupted her thought and pushed her behind him, since angels were invisible to humans unless he was seen.

Her fingers itched to slide her knife into the man's belly for the torture he'd caused Ananiel. Instead, she used a compulsion spell to make him come inside. "Four, three, two..."

He opened the door.

"*Exteotum Elemenortus,*" A tangled, pink, glowing corkscrew mist surrounded him. Moira erased his memory and unwound the ward on Ananiel. "The spell you've cast is reversed and null, the spirit returned to his flesh. I have banished the curse into nothingness and erased the power of evil. Moira stayed calm, making sure her words hit their mark.

Chapter Twenty-Nine

ANANIEL

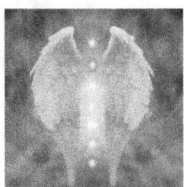

The incapacitating impact of Norman's magical ward slammed me harder than the turbulent rainfall pounding the rippling seas. A hate-bomb ticked inside me, waiting to explode. The moment my etheric aura entered my body, I visualized how I'd tear to shreds the warlock bastard when I got my hands on him. Erasing the trident mark from my skin would seem like a scraped knee after I skewered him over Hades' pitchfork and watched him burn alive for an eternity. Still, the punishment would not suffice for his diabolical crimes.

Samael's belly laugh pierced my rambling thoughts.

"Get out of my head," I sneered with a savage intensity.

"Ananiel's return, fiercer than ever." Samael moved out of the circle, allowing me room to regain my awareness.

I leaned on my right elbow, confused at why my body lay in a bramble of sea grasses. Overhead, the moonlight trickled through the leafy canopy. Salty, sweet apricot mixed with the sea scents of the estuary brought thoughts of lovemaking with Grace, her submission, and the trident markings. I stared into Samael's dark eyes and smiled. Of all the fallen angels to save me. "How'd you destroy the poison eating my flesh?"

"The warlock used dark necromancer magic. He intended for you to live without form."

Uriel handed me the Sword of Wrath, a long infantry rapier with a thin blade. "You must rise and fulfill your destiny. Time runs against us. Retrieve the sacral carnelian scarab."

The roar of the ocean rang in my brain. I hated leaving Grace a second longer in the clutches of that son-of-a-bitch, no-good bastard Norman. "I must hurry and retrieve the gem and return to the White House and help Grace."

"Aah, you're blinded with fury and do not see what is before you. Your destiny was never to be at the White House. The issue with the shifter realm and its problems are of little concern to the choir of angels."

"She's my archeia." I raised an arm in the air with the wrath of vengeance on my mind.

"Then get your head out of your ass, settle down that wrath of yours, and direct your powers through your mind, not your fist."

Uriel's own rage shook me to the core.

Samael cocked his brow at Uriel. "Tone it down."

"He must complete the kundalini, or my child will die."

My gaze darted to Moira's stomach then back to Uriel. "Do the choir of angels know?"

"Not all. Many feel the Sarim princes are Yahweh's chosen because of our lineage. They resent our unique position amongst the heavens. Many despise the fallen angels and their children."

The flame of justice fired in Uriel's speckled green eyes. He raised a fist in strength. His torch and the flaming sword crawled beneath his skin in preparation for battle. His fear for Moira and our brothers was apparent by the eagerness of his weapons to emerge.

I rubbed the jagged scar under my left pectoral muscle, right above my heart. I'd lost so much when I followed my brother into the mortal realm of the celestial pantheon. I'd not returned to Kumuria, our celestial home, since that fateful day. Instead, I'd chosen to live out my destiny as protector of the discarded angelic children of the Grigori, the watchers who'd given mankind knowledge against the will of the gods.

I turned to Samael. He'd committed the greatest sin according to the angelic choir. He'd planted the tree of knowledge and encouraged Eve to partake of the forbidden fruit. Those accusing me said I gave secrets to humanity because I craved power, just like Samael.

"What now?" I fought back the rage to go after Grace and be done with the constant bickering between those wanting control. But we, as Yahweh created us, had to choose sides again, just like in the first rebellion. As leader of the Grigori watchers, I had an obligation to the nephilim and humans.

Samael's golden wings expanded. His breastplate appeared along with the vambraces that cloaked his forearms.

Uriel followed suit.

Without hesitation, I did the same. Our wings filtered out the moonlight, creating a shield of protection that encircled the baby within the womb. The firstborn of the archangels and their archeia spirit mates represented a new beginning, and a chance for a fresh start.

The aching sorrow of revenge soured me like an old festering wound, while the others spoke of a future, of hope, of dreams and of a more compatible universe. I'd protected, trained, and taught the Nephilim children to expect this new age. If I failed, the kundalini dragon would submerge into the dark age of time, destroying the universal light.

I looked up and gazed at the nearly full moon. There were only twenty-four hours until a total lunar eclipse and the night of the wolf blood moon. A night where new wolf pairings rejoiced in their union.

Moira's soft fingers brushed my cheek. "The baby and I are counting on you." She reached into her pouch and removed the two drachma coins. "You'll need these to enter Olympus and ride the hippocampi into Poseidon's Castle."

"Any idea where the gemstone lives?" I took the drachma coins, placing them in my pouch.

A chuckle came from Uriel. "Think of the stallion and mare."

"Demeter." I cocked my brow, remembering how Poseidon tricked Demeter into his bed.

"I bet they'll be mixed within the coral and gemstones of his castle floors," Samael said.

"Right in plain sight." Uriel agreed.

How long had the sacral carnelian stone been in Poseidon's possession? The fates had a funny way of directing one's life.

The angelic energy soared through my body, healing my physique, my thoughts, and my powers. I visualized my trident, and it appeared in my hand. The trident would lead me to Olympus, the land of the Greek gods. "Samael, a new growth in humanity's history awaits. I would be honored to have you beside me during any conflict.

"We're angels of wrath, and it will be our duty to pass judgement against those who have wronged humanity."

"Like Jacobson?" Uriel gave Samael a resentful glance. Samael and Uriel had made a past wager, and as a result, they sent an innocent man to Tartarus because Lilith demanded Samael appease her desire to test man's faith.

Yahweh's golden light shone above, his sword raised toward the moonlight. The glory of his stature overshadowed our own fire.

Uriel, angel of the moon, rose on our father's right side.

Samael and I, part of the fallen angels, stood with our free will being tested.

The minute hand of time ticked. I lived an eternity of lives in one mortal moment. Both Samael and I raised our swords.

"May the darkness change into light."

I realized my experience had led me to this precise moment in history, where the divide between worlds rested on the free will of the Sarim princes.

Without preamble, my wings receded, and I left the estuary still filled with Grace's faint scent. Once outside the cove, a clarity of mind calmed the wrath soaring through me, and I focused on what I needed to do.

I had to find Norman and David's weaknesses and bring them to justice before the American people. The evil warlocks' destruction must rise from their own dark seeds of revenge.

Chapter Thirty

GRACE

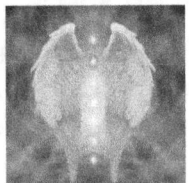

Hot water splayed across my shoulders, massaging the hard knots of stress, but no amount of water could wash away the turmoil seething inside my soul.

Norman sat at the desk, waiting. His constant presence sickened me with every glance, word, or gesture he made.

Yesterday, after I returned from my workout, Norman trailed after me. He attended a morning meeting with my chief of staff, and a special breakfast with congressional leaders. By lunchtime, I'd had enough of his harassment. The humiliation of pretending to be his wife soured my stomach to the point of total disgust. Just one more day of the charade and I'd have him arrested, but until then, I couldn't risk losing everything I'd worked for.

There was a knock on the door. "What?" I snapped.

"Hurry! Your briefing with the CIA secretary is in fifteen minutes," Norman said.

"Notify his secretary that my security chief of staff will join us this morning."

A low snort came through the door. "She is aware of your request."

I hadn't found a quiet moment without Norman or David being

attached to me like glue. I released a breath and could only hope Leslie had warned my brothers.

Yesterday, the shifter council of the Northeast district and pack leaders around the country offered substantial evidence to the Senate hearings. Today, the Senate would vote either to pass or to reject the legislation.

I ran my fingers through my hair to rinse out the soap. I'd worked throughout my presidency for this moment to establish the shifter's birthrights within our country. If the Senate rejected an open discussion, we stood to face another conflict much like the Native American fight for territory. In this time in history, manifest destiny wasn't on the side of the mortals but lay with the shifters.

Turning the water off, I reached for the towel and thought about Ananiel. I hoped someone found the message I'd sent through the chute. As grief settled thick and suffocating in my soul, I closed my eyes. The sigil signature between Ananiel and me grew weak. Fear coursed through my body that his brothers might be too late to save him.

Dropping the towel to the floor, I recited a poem for courage to help me with the challenges facing my day. I slipped into a sleeveless spandex unitard and then donned the outfit with a taupe pencil skirt and sports jacket. I chose each piece of clothing so that I could remove it easily.

I slipped into a pair of black pumps, ready to face the unavoidable task of endless meetings.

Another pounding on my door, but this time Norman didn't wait for my answer and barged in.

I turned with a cheeky smile and walked right past him into the living area where David paced.

I had a terrible feeling regarding David. More than distrust, downright disgust came from him. What did he have against the shifters?

The covens throughout the United States usually dealt effectively with the mage communities. What puzzled me was how David expected to avoid sanctions once his crimes became public knowledge?

Norman and David stayed behind, unable to attend the presidential briefings.

I sighed with relief, giving me a moment of reprieve. Even alone, I had an uncanny feeling Norman had found a method to still be present. I slid the ring off my left finger. I had little intention of wearing it in these important meetings. Today, he'd learn I'd broken the ring's power, using Moira's satchel of magically enhanced stones. The ring no longer bound my gifts, and after the vote, it didn't matter. I rubbed the locket between my fingers, thankful for my mother's ancient magic.

Juna moved in beside me and handed me a briefing folder.

I opened it and thumbed through the pages.

Brothers notified.

Men in black stationed inside the FBI building.

Ananiel is safe and alive. He'll return during the blood moon and take back what's his.

My trembling hand clutched the slip of paper even tighter.

"He survived." I wanted to bury myself in pleasure to enjoy the moment, but I kept my expression stony, revealing nothing of my thoughts.

"He's mad as hell." The edge of her mouth crooked into a knowing grin.

I tilted my head, and our gazes met with understanding. I wanted to ask her more, but too much was at stake as I handed back the folder. "Thank you." I tapped twice on the folder, our code of communication to each other.

My secretary hustled in with a stack of papers.

The nerves in my stomach coiled into a knot. Even the Zoloft I'd taken this morning didn't push away the anxiety. The moment I'd fought to achieve—for so long would happen this morning. The Senate would either reject or pass the most important legislation since the Civil Rights Act of the 1960s.

Our determination to usurp the shifter hunters depended on everything falling into place today. Every alpha across the United States waited inside the offices of the shifter council. I shuffled through the stack of memos and tried to focus on the task before me.

Next, I headed to the Roosevelt Room to meet with a branch of the Paranormal Investigative Agency of the CIA.

"Good day, President Isaeva," Jim Stewart, directorate of the PIA, offered his hand.

"Thank you for attending on such short notice."

After I took my seat, the other representatives, along with the three Norn wolves, took their respective chairs.

Juna stood behind me with two men on either side of us.

My secretary passed around prospective updates on the hunters.

"What news have you uncovered?" I asked, gazing around the room to gauge the reactions of each person.

"The Montana wildlife refuge has ties to individuals who might be responsible for the attack in Wyoming. Our current intelligence produced information that, occasionally, wildcats and wolves are used in wealthy hunter games. Our investigators traced the money back to the refuge, but then the source disappeared. The leaders are aware of the NSA investigation on behalf of the FBI. I suspect they've gone underground until the heat dies down." The directorate's gaze stopped on each person.

"I agree," stated Sebastian, the leader of the Norn wolf clan, certainty in his words. "That's why we'll go in as rogue outsiders."

"Next steps." I lowered my shoulders, my lips pinching in disgust at the cruelty of hunters to kill innocent women and children.

"We've evidence Norman Hollered is a member of the refuge," Vlad said. "Romulus and I will infiltrate the organization until we reach the top man, then we'll gather enough evidence to convict these monsters."

"Excellent. What should I report to the alphas?" I turned to the table and leaned back as they tossed ideas around like Ping-pong balls. I found my thoughts drifting to the congressional hearings. My palms grew moist waiting for the results of the Senate vote. Listening to the directors grew more difficult as the minute hand ticked slower than the sands of an hourglass.

Finally, Jim Stewart turned and handed me a file with recommendations. "The alpha leaders expect the truth."

"Agreed. Will any CIA members go undercover?" I asked.

"No. If we act impulsively, we'll overplay our hand and never catch the actual killers behind the hideous murders."

"The men the FBI arrested at the scene ... I assume they'll face criminal charges?"

"If they don't disappear. Their lawyers convinced the judge to allow them out on bail."

A strong sense of revenge rippled through me. If ever I wanted to use the death magic, it was on these hunters who killed for sport. My wolf's growl reminded me of the consequence of a rash action. Even righteous beliefs can falter with dark intentions.

Juna took a subtle step closer to me.

My internal wolf's ears metaphorically perked, hearing her slight movement. I turned toward her and tapped my forefinger twice on the table, letting her know I was fine. With the blood moon days away, my silver wolf needed to run. She wanted to finish the mating ritual. After the removal of the mark, I struggled to fight the frenzy. A burning wave of nausea poured over me. I clutched my belly and doubled over.

"A five-minute break?" The director offered with concern on his face.

"Yes." I stood and returned to the Oval Office. With all my energy, I reached within my core and pulled at the sigil spell. I sensed Ananiel's love for me and clung to the belief he'd stop Norman from claiming what he considered his rights.

A tap sounded on the door. "Are you alright?" Juna asked.

"I'm fine. Tell my secretary to refill the coffee and teapot."

"Will do."

I washed my hands, letting the warm water soothe my heart. Memories of the night in the estuary and the marking of my mate filled me with hope for a brighter future. The trident was so fitting for an angel of wrath who loved the raging sea. I traced the three prongs on the palm of my hand. No one could take his love from me, not even an evil warlock. I looked in the mirror, staring at my reflection. Silver flecks sparkled in the green of my eyes. *I know you miss him too.*

I returned to the Roosevelt Room. "Gentlemen, pardon my need for a break. Please refresh your drinks, and we'll finish our meeting."

The next hour passed, and the committee exited the White House. Satisfied that a new policy existed to protect the shifter territories put me at ease.

Jim Stewart, the director, had displayed an understanding and sensitivity for which I was grateful. Now, I could turn my attention to the Senate hearings.

Juna and I stepped into the study next to the Oval Office and turned on the television to watch the congressional chamber proceedings. We both knew what this vote meant to the shifter tribes.

I drew in a deep breath. If all our carefully laid plans worked, the road before me looked promising.

Chapter Thirty-One

GRACE

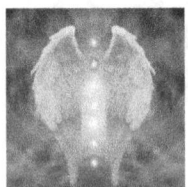

Sitting in the study off the Oval Office, I stared at the large television screen, watching each senator vote. I locked my hands together saying a silent prayer that the legislation passed the Senate floor. Two votes to win.

Senator Thomas: "Yea."

Senator Jordon: "Nay"

The last to decide. I bit my bottom lip. If this bill failed and shifters were denied citizenship, I truly believed a chasm between our species threatened to separate us.

Senator Loren: "Yea."

Tears of relief filled my soul.

The Senate passed the amendment making all United States born shifters citizens. Finally, the people would have all the civil rights and liberties of any natural-born individual. With the remote control, I turned off the television and lifted the handset of the phone to my ear. "Connect me to the shifter council direct redline."

Two rings, three rings before the director answered the phone. "Director Hobbs."

"Hi, Hobbs."

"Good afternoon Madame President. I assume you're calling concerning the favorable vote."

"We won." Tears slid down my cheeks. I'd helped my mother's people to gain the rights they deserved.

"If you hadn't committed your time and resources this day would be far into the future."

"The only hurdle to cross is my identity. Will the American people feel portrayed to learn I'm a shifter? My whole life I denied my identity to fit into a system that embraced a narrow view of thinking."

Hobbs paused, one minute, two. "Will you run for a second term?"

"No. I've decided to use my leadership inside the shifter bureau."

"I'll be honored to work with you. The challenges we faces will take compassion, calm, and a collective mind set to navigate the future.

"Thank you, Thomas." I ended the call. A rippling tide of joy raced through me. I couldn't wait to face the nation and embrace who I was.

"I'll be in the Rose garden." I told my secretary.

Leaving my desk, I exited through the Oval Office and out into the fresh air. Relief washed over me. We won. The gardens would be a perfect place to hold an immediate press conference to the public. Being so close to the end of my term, I still couldn't believe the legislation received enough votes and passed.

Long-buried emotions stirred within me, including the need to find justice and help my mama's pack. Mama, you'd be proud. I succeeded in protecting our people. Joyful tears trickled along my cheeks. I wished Ananiel was here to share this momentous occasion. I shook my hands in the air and danced a jig. *I did it!*

I settled under the willow tree and let the tension leave my soul. Things would work out. This evening I'd address the nation and congratulate all who helped to bring this historic moment to fruition. Belief in our country's goodness reaffirmed itself today. My heart filled with hope.

A flock of birds heading south flew overhead. Soon the November election and, the moment of truth. Was I ready to govern the shifters? Part of me sought the refuge of peace, but now was no time to stop the fight. The future looked bright, and the alpha packs needed a trail-blazer they could trust. A leader who believed in equality for all. I sighed with relief, closed my eyes, and escaped into the cool breeze of autumn.

"President Isaeva." Ms. Lawerence shook my arm. "Wake-up. An explosion occurred at the Hoover building."

I dashed for the Oval Office and froze as news flashed across the screen. Firetrucks surrounded the whole complex. One side of the brick building was demolished.

"An explosion happened around 2:40 this afternoon at the Hoover complex. At last count, twenty people are trapped inside a fourth-floor conference room of the northeast offices of the shifter council. Firefighters have pulled out four victims said to have died in the explosion."

The Aiden pack and twelve other regional leaders were inside waiting for the vote. My palms grew wet. My brother's and the cadets were there. I had to do something. This couldn't be happening. Congress signed the legislation. Everything was supposed to be all right.

The hunters. The hunters were responsible. Nothing made sense, just a rambling list of things I had to do.

"Where's Norman?" I asked my secretary. No doubt he and his brother had something to do with the explosion. He'd fought the legislation's passage, destroyed my mark, hated the shifters, and soon, he'd pay for what he'd done to the American people.

"I need a car. Call me a damn car!" The hysteria grew stronger every minute. Another two people were carried out on stretchers.

"Calm down, Ms. Isaeva. Ms. Price is on her way."

I stood in place, watching as flames engulfed the third floor. My calm was close to shattering. I had to keep my shit together. The American people would expect an explanation. Just a few minutes ago, I was so proud of our accomplishments, but now the fragile agreements threatened to divide the species deeper than before. I covered my mouth and choked on a sob of disbelieving grief. Three more people dead.

Secret Service secured the doors and offices. Juna took my arm and moved me through the throngs of security and staff. "Come with me." She dragged me out of the Oval Office, through the Roosevelt Room, and into a storage closet. "Dustin was caught in the explosion."

The hitch in her voice scared me.

"Is he all right?" A dark fear coiled in the pit of my stomach. She'd brought me to this room. Something bad. "Dustin. Is he...?"

"I don't know. Most of the dead have been mortals. The shifters healed themselves or we'd be dealing with many more deaths."

A fragile flame of hope moved inside me.

"Who's responsible?" I gripped her arm feeling the anger rise.

"We don't know yet."

"I do. Norman and that sick fuck of a brother."

"Where are they now? Yesterday, he followed me with his nose up my ass, and today he's preoccupied, suddenly unavailable."

"His sister's been kidnapped."

I tried to restrain the scream that ballooned upward. Sheila, his sister, had been brutally raped and left for dead five years ago. I hadn't thought much about her since she lived mostly with David and Norman. Rarely did she leave the protection of her caretakers. Now I was puzzled, I'd been positive Norman was behind the destruction.

"He is." Ananiel flashed into the closet.

I flung my arms around his neck and sniffed battling the tears that seeped from under my closed eyelids. "Take me to my brothers." I withdrew from his embrace and reached for the door, but he pulled me back into his arms.

"Roger and the other shifters are safe. The nephilim are saving as many mortals lives as they can."

"Where's Dustin?"

Ananiel gripped me even tighter. "He didn't make it."

My heart tightened painfully in my chest. "What?" As I pulled back to refute his words. All sound lodged in my throat along with my heart.

Ananiel cupped the back of my head and pressed my face against his chest. His thundering heart pounded in my ears.

"Dustin was at the epicenter of the explosion, along with the Louisiana alpha. So far, they're the only shifters we've lost."

Revulsion filled me and I shifted into my wolf. I snarled in Ananiel's direction, determined to find Norman and tear every shred of him to pieces. He'd killed my brother and shattered all hope of a peaceful resolution.

"Shift back," Ananiel's firm voice demanded.

I didn't care anymore. Everything was ruined. I wouldn't be that same scared girl back when the explosion killed my parents. Childhood memories cooked in the juices of my hate.

Ananiel reached for me.

I snipped his hand, needing to get out of the room.

"Her eyes have gone feral. Bring her back."

I heard the terror in Juna's voice.

"Submit."

Ananiel's voice was low, masculine, and oh-so-sure-of-himself blocking the door.

Juna circled from behind me and joined Ananiel. She pointed a taser at me.

"Submit!" His tone held no mercy and his eyes burned red with fury. "Submit now!"

My body shifted and I lay naked on the floor. My clothes a pile of shredded material.

Ananiel snatched me by the hair, pulled me to my feet and kissed me, linking our sigil magick together.

"Let me go." A growl left my throat. I glowered at him, ready to escape if he opened the door.

"Not gonna happen, baby girl."

"That's my brother." I braced myself against him, still furious with the need to taste Norman's blood.

"In thirty minutes, you need to go on national television and give the biggest speech of your life. You must calm the shifters and humans alike."

With his arm wrapped around my shoulder, he held me in an iron grip.

Juna was on my other side.

"Keep the taser on her until I return with clothes in case she shifts back. Where are the caramel chews that help with your anxiety?"

"In my top drawer. In the right side of my closet you'll see a blue dress. Bring it."

"Count to ten. Relax. We don't have much time. I promise you this isn't how you want the public to see you," Ananiel's soothing words coaxed me to stay calm.

"Just hurry, standing here in the nude's rather uncomfortable." The heat of embarrassment fused my cheeks.

Juna cocked her brow.

I recognized a faint glint of pity in her eyes.

"You doing o'kay?" She still kept the taser pointed at me.

"I lost control, for a moment...put the gun away. I'm alright."

"I'll wait until Ananiel returns."

I couldn't blame her, seeing a feral wolf snarling with a mouth of teeth would be the strongest of people on alert.

Ananiel flashed carrying my outfit and black pumps.

I dressed. "Let's go."

"Anyone who sees me will think I'm one of the Secret Service. Stay close until I get you back to safety."

Leslie came through the throngs of people surrounding the entrance to the Oval Office. She ran towards me, but was stopped by the secret service. Kai, took Leslie by the arm and followed me into my private study.

"Are you all right?" Leslie threw her arms around me.

The last of my resolve left me. I let the tears pour down my cheeks and flood me with the anguish ripping apart my heart. "I'll never be all right again," I sobbed.

Ananiel sat me on the couch, grabbed a warm cloth from the bathroom, and wiped my face. "Pull yourself together." He kissed me. "You are an alpha female, strong and powerful."

I reached for a tissue, wiped my eyes, and blew my nose. "I'm the leader of the United States. The people depend on my guidance."

"That's my girl," Ananiel ruffled my hair. "Leslie, I need you to go to the press room and take charge. Offer them exclusives, if you have to, but I do not want the press pushing their mics in her face after she addresses the nation."

"Will you accompany me?" I asked Ananiel.

"The American people think you are married to Norman, and for the moment, the situation has to stay that way."

A slight tremor belied his feelings. The tender innocuous tone of his voice broke my resolve to stay angry. I kissed him with every promise of love that stirred in my heart.

"I told the press the marriage was a farce. Why would they assume any different?"

"The media suppressed the statement," Leslie stated with a grim tone to her voice. "The reporters, along with me, thought you were hiding a deeper secret."

"And you didn't stand behind me?" Sarcasm littered every word. My own best friend hadn't believed me.

"I thought you'd turned your back against me and your family. Running off and getting married alone."

"It never happened!" I wanted to tear out my hair and scream it to the world.

"Norman uses the leverage he has to keep you under his control. He knows if you show up with me and announce we are mates, your reputation and credibility will be destroyed." Ananiel lifted my chin. "You're the United States President, it will take courage to lead in the tumultuous time facing the nation."

Conflicting emotions swirled around in my thoughts, "I can't do it without you." I dropped my head and took his hand to my lips, kissing him as if this would be the last time I saw him. "I love you."

"We'll get through this mess. Just hang on." His fingers thrummed through my hair. "I promise."

"How will you stop Norman from hurting me before I have a chance to tell the American public?

"I have his sister." His eyes narrowed.

"Sheila?" My own eyes widened in utter horror.

Ananiel stood. "I had no choice."

"Using her is wrong." Her damaged soul didn't deserve to be dragged through the drudgery we all experienced.

A knock came on the door, and my secretary poked her head inside. "Ms. Isaeva, you go live in three minutes."

I rushed to the mirror.

"Wash your face and I'll help with your make-up." Leslie tugged at my arm.

I sat on the toilet seat, wiping a cloth over my face.

"Pucker your lips." Two of her fingers swiped a quick cover-up of foundation, and then brushed my cheeks with blush. "This will have to do. Put on some lipstick."

Ananiel's stood in the doorway. "I'm sorry."

"Just go!" I turned away, still angry he'd stooped to their level. "Kidnapping an innocent girl to gain power over a political rival isn't what I expected from a Sarim prince, protector of humanity. Go! I don't need your kind of help."

As I opened the door to the Oval Office, he flashed and left me alone to handle the media.

I took the seat behind my desk and looked soberly into the camera.

Juna, Kai, and Leslie blended in with the other reporters standing in the rear of the room.

"In the last hour, tragedy has struck our nation. The Hoover Center experienced an explosion killing ten American citizens. My brother, Dustin Isaeva, and Gerald Fry of the shifter council, along with six FBI members of the shifter agency and two office staff. We at the White House grieve with the family members for their loss."

The words caught in my throat, and I struggled to finish the sentence. Norman, my aunt, and my uncle stood in the rear of the room. Annoyance was written all over Norman's face. He must have guessed or figured out Ananiel had his sister.

In this, I couldn't blame his rage, but he deserved the pits of hell for what he'd done to me and the threats over my family. I returned my gaze to the camera. "Todays important civil rights legislation passed in the Senate. I will sign into law the most valued and important declaration of the twenty-first century."

A round of applause sounded and the cameras turned off.

"I'll speak with the media in the press room."

My spine stiffened as I walked up to Norman. I touched my locket and said a silent prayer. All gazes on me, I took the ring off my finger and handed it to him. "Your ward's been broken, now get out of the White House before I have you arrested on conspiracy charges."

His look of hatred grew, and he slanted his eyes with a death stare meant to chill me to the bone.

My fear left me. This warlock used me, had killed my brother, and created a division between species that would take me years to repair.

"Don't do this." Aunt Cheryl reached for my arm.

I turned and faced her. Years of buried lies and cruelties flooded my mind. Her criticism of me, and the denial of my identity. The constant erasing of my mother. The lies regarding the explosion that left me buried alive and killed my parents. The truth filled me with an ache of loss for everything that I'd denied about myself, and now, my brother was gone.

"You knew all along. You knew who Norman was and what he intended to do."

"This is not the place to discuss family business." My uncle faced me.

He looked so much like his brother, my father. My father had left his family for my mother, a shifter. They'd been in love and so determined to make a life for themselves.

"I have a job to do." I turned to Juna. "Escort these three off the White House grounds and alert security immediately."

"Our relationship isn't over, Grace."

"Accept the loss, Norman."

"The American public will demand your resignation when they learn you're really a shifter."

I froze. A camera clicked and flashes filled the room. The moment of truth arrived.

I drew in a deep breath and walked out, knowing tongues would wag. I'd have to find a way to spin this news to the press and minimize the damage.

Chapter Thirty-Two

ANANIEL

I clung Sheila's hand like a child. It pained me to take her from her home, but Norman only understood brute strength. We arrived at Archipelago Island. "Sheila, this is Sophia and Ariel. They'll take you to their house to play with their two daughters."

"Will they play Barbies with me?"

Sophia reached down and smoothed the woman's shiny brunette curls. "Yes we will. Do you like brownies? We can make a batch this afternoon."

She clapped her hands together. "I do."

"Come along with me."

"Will my brothers pick me up at your house?"

"I promise you they will pick you up after your visit with my girls." Sophia nodded for me to leave.

Ariel and I left Sheila with Sophia. We flashed to my office so we could speak in private.

"How many lives lost in the explosion?" Ariel asked.

"Ten. Dustin didn't make it. He, along with three others, were at the epicenter during the explosion. Not much was left of their bodies."

"Any loss of nephilim?" Ariel's voice trailed off into nothingness.

"Louisiana alpha, the rest were mortal." Ariel took a seat in one of the arm chairs in my sitting room.

"How's Grace?"

"Troubled."

"She's in shock. After the mating is over and the kundalini dragon hangs in the sky, she'll understand."

Jeffrey knocked then brought in a tray. "Sophia mentioned you might need some coffee." He poured each of us a mug. "Your archeia's message is what saved your life. I'm impressed she thought to send me a note through your private chute."

"I'm eternally grateful for your quick thinking. Jeffrey."

"Thank you, sir." He left.

Drinking our coffee, I took a moment to gather my thoughts. "I'll be needing a favor."

"I'll do what I can."

"If you don't hear from me or see the Kundalini Dragon by sunrise, use the chute inside my shower and bring Grace to the island. Her life could be in serious danger."

"No problem. If all is well, I'll have Sophia plan a celebration dinner."

The kundalini had no way of rising if we didn't pledge our bodies during the exact moment of the eclipse. The ritualistic claiming would tie our blood links together and make our spirits one.

Ariel added a spoonful of sugar to his coffee.

Gavin came in and pulled up another chair.

I turned to Gavin. "Tonight's the full moon eclipse. I've thwarted Norman for the moment, but I need you to send spies to the surface. Tag his and his brother's every movement. They're both powerful warlocks. No doubt they're pissed I have Sheila."

"Kai's already placed more security around Grace. She's attached a unit on both men."

"Good." I sipped my coffee ready to complete the final lap.

"You have a few hours before the rise of the full moon. Go and retrieve the sacral carnelian scarab and fulfill your destiny." Ariel sighed and leaned forward. "I'll take Sheila to my home in Oregon. She'll be safe with my girls. If all goes as planned, we'll send her home first thing in the morning."

"Thank you." I rose and dismissed them to return to their duties.

I flashed to the landing and climbed in the chute heading to the Olympian pantheon and the city of Olympia.

I approached the golden gates and paid the drachma coin to the Horai goddess who guarded the gates into the ancient acropolis. Inside the golden gates, I wasted no time and flashed to the Aegean Sea.

Using a conch shell, I called Poseidon's half-fish and half-horse hippocampi, to carry me to the palace. Each minute felt like an eternity as time ticked faster and faster. I placed the seashell horn to my mouth and called the rage of the wind. The swells of the waves slammed in violent crashes mirroring the terror I experienced deep in my soul.

The sigil of magic binding Grace seared into me. An anguish tore through her and I sensed her pain. Images surfaced of David drinking her light, and stealing the magic of her spirit.

The scar beneath my breast split and a trickle of blood oozed down my chest. Dark magic swirled around our sigil connection searching for a way to sever the bond.

"Stormy."

Her safe word echoed in my mind and I fought not to give in and flash to her side.

"Fight back. I expect you to follow your alpha's command. Now, fight."

"Hurry, my archangel."

Until the final mating Grace would suffer the frenzy of the lunar eclipse and risked exposure to the mortals. An urgency filled me and my impatience soared. I thrust my anger into the sea, forcing a whirlpool to form, almost sucking in the hippocampi's approaching the shoreline.

I inserted the coin inside the rein pouch connected to the hippocampus and placed one foot on each of the shoulder blades and took the harness in my hands. The sea's walls rose, creating a path to the sea floor and Poseidon's castle.

A bellowing voice vibrated throughout the sound waves of the sea. Atop his head he wore his wreath of wild celery leaves. His thick white hair fell across his shoulders like wave caps cresting the breakers. "Welcome."

I slid in beside his chariot and let the reins fall from my hands. "I'm here for the sacral carnelian scarab."

"I've been expecting you, Storm Watcher. How is your archeia faring with her newfound powers?"

"The Celtic witch used the open portal to escape her prison. The bitch sends her love."

Poseidon bellowed, and the earth shook under his roar. "I will tear her limb by limb when I find the witch."

"You'll have to stand in line. She helped the warlocks remove the trident from Graces flesh allowing another to claim her during the blood moon."

We headed toward the castle's entrance.

"You have little time to waste." Poseidon gave me a pointed looked.

"Ten people died during at explosion at the Hoover building."

"Shifters?"

"Two."

"I've taken Norman's sister. She's hidden on the island."

"A wise bargaining chip. That's his Achilles' heel."

"If you have the sacral carnelian scarab, I'll take the stone. Grace's in trouble. She attempts to hide her anguish, but it grows stronger as the full moon rises."

Poseidon waved his hands toward his great hall. "I know not of where the Moirae have hidden them. They are amongst the coral and gems that layer the castle floors. The fates foretold of your future. Only you, my treasured watcher, will know their location."

"The games the fates play with our minds is worse than the Isthmian games of the gods."

Poseidon chuckled. "Yeah, I've had my challenges with the sisters. They enjoy twisting a man's insides to the point of insanity."

"Any clue?"

"Sacral is the sex chakra. Check-out the seduction chamber where I've taken many a willing female to sate my needs."

"That's a start." We leave the foyer and head toward a winding staircase of various rooms used to entertain the gods in their pursuit of pleasure.

"You are the angel of wrath, just invalidate the magick used to protect the gems. The answer seems quite simple to me."

I hustled to the center of the foyer and called to the Moirae, the three sisters of fate in the Greek pantheon. "What is the sigil to invalidate the magic used to protect the gems?"

I concentrated and opened my mind, allowing the goddesses to heed my call. If they favored my journey, they would bless me with an answer. If not, the kundalini's resurrection failed this very night.

"Sharphiel."

"Got it."

In focusing on my emotions, I needed to block the chaos filling my heart. Slowly, the floor swirled in a counterclockwise motion throughout the palace. I moved from place to place until I reached the room with the depiction of the great fall of angels. I followed Lucifer, the bringer of light, to the human realm that day. The day I became the leader of the Grigori watchers. On the day, I brought knowledge to the new mortals.

In the far corner of the room, a window overlooked a lush garden of blue lotus flowers. A nymph voice whispered, and I recited the sigil 'sharphiel' eleven times as she instructed. Within the valley of flowers, a ribbon of magic snaked its way through the archway window into the grand room.

I follow as the bluish smoke weaves throughout the halls of the passage, down a long corridor, and into Poseidon's queen's chamber.

Amphitrite stood among a floor of corals and shimmering pearls. She opened her palms, and the spiral of color poured into her hands then disappeared.

I bowed to one knee in reverence to the sea goddess. "Amphitrite, it honors my heart to be welcomed onto island."

Like the other nereids, her gowns were layers of beautiful silks, so seductive to the eyes of men. The lyric of her sea nymph's voice eased the howl of the wind, bringing calm to the seas.

"Storm Watcher, protector of the nephilim, you seek the sacral carnelian scarab that belongs to the kundalini dragon. I've kept the sacral carnelian scarab hidden, waiting for the day of their resurrection."

Raising my head to take in the beauty of her light, I nodded. "Do you have the stone? The moon rises in the celestial human cities. My archeia awaits my return."

Seahorses whispered in the queen's ear. "In payment for the gems I require you bring your nephilim warriors and compete in the Isthmian games representing Poseidon and me."

"I am the Grigori leader. Not a god, but one of the Sarim princes. The power to guarantee the nephilim will compete is beyond my rights."

"You humble yourself, great Storm Watcher of the seas. This pleases me."

"Thank you goddess."

"When you return to Oceania and the guild, remind your water nephilim of what's at stake, for the battle of light is just beginning. The destiny of many will be decided on the outcome of the winners."

I arched my brow, eager to return to Grace. "I will do as you ask. In honor of the sea, I pledge my loyalty and agree to compete in honor of the water god of the Olympian pantheon."

"Yahweh will not be pleased," Amphitrite moved close and traced the trident embedded in my armor. "Why do you chance angering him by giving your loyalty to Poseidon?"

I removed my breast plate and tunic to reveal the scar reddened with droplets of blood. "My father caused this curse and I've paid the price."

"Is that all?"

I knew what she meant but fought the feelings that soared through me. The trident branded me, and when Norman used magic to remove the mark, my heart shattered inside. "Grace is my archeia. I love her." I never expected to open myself to the intense pain of losing her, but I had.

Amphitrite stepped around me. "Come with me, angel of wrath. You, like Poseidon never notice what is right before your eyes."

Poseidon entered the chamber and my brows rose in amusement. I followed her to the trident nestled in the corner. She picked up the harpoon and swiped her hand over the thill in long loving strokes.

The goddess gave Poseidon a sizzling look that caused my own cock to react.

A low, seductive laugh escaped her.

Poseidon winked and walked to his throne. In the palm of her hand, the orange carnelian stone glowed with a powerful sensuality.

She handed me the gem. "Go to your Grace. Reuniting the shifters will take courage and patience. She will need your protection, for the road will be rife with challenges."

"We'll make it." I gave her a hopeful glance.

"The night is not over."

Chapter Thirty-Three

GRACE

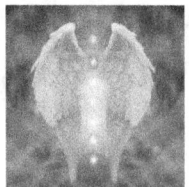

After the police finished their investigation, most of the shifters left the D.C. area and returned to their packs. With the press surrounding the White House, I couldn't even grieve Dustin's life.

In the morning, I'd face the nation and state that I'd not be running for a second term.

My wolf's need to run wild filled me with anguish and a terrible feeling of loss. Never in my life did I expect to take part in one of the moon celebrations, but now my body screamed with need.

I locked my private quarters and shifted to fight off the ache between my legs. The moon brought on the frenzy, and I couldn't fight my sexual hunger. Shifting back, I headed to the shower for some release.

Tonight, in the deep recesses of the forest, hundreds of shifters throughout the world would celebrate this special ceremonial claiming of their mates. A lucky time of unity between packs. Now is the time for couples to receive the blessing. The pack honored children born under its power.

Drinking a cup of hot tea, I curled on the couch in a loose-fitting shirt and sweats. Juna and Kai both guarded my door. A tribe of others surrounded the gardens and any other entrance into the residence. I laid my head on the cushion, fighting the gray that threatened to invade my heart. When Yahweh gave me the gift of color, he warned me to avoid the cold emptiness of dark gray magic.

I fought the ribbons coiling around me, but the threads intertwined my six senses. My mouth tightened in irritation as my fists pushed into my temples trying to get the migraine to go away.

The incessant knocking made my head hurt worse. I rose to my feet, expecting Leslie. The door opened and Juna lay knocked out on the floor. David pointed her weapon at me. I pushed the emergency button on my phone alerting the security team.

"Leave your hands where I can see them." The phone dropped to the floor. The idea of pulling my knife and gutting him impossible.

His heavy scowl was a definite sign of his anger. Curling his fingers around my upper arm, he latched onto my breath, absorbing my life essence. I couldn't think or figure out what to do. When he released his hold, I dropped to my knees and reached for my throat thirsty for air. Black spots danced in front of my eyes as I struggled for breath.

"Where's my sister?"

Barely able to escape his onslaught, I crawled over to the emergency tab to alert Kai.

Before I could reach, he grabbed my wrists and cuffed them together. "I've a mage taking care of the problem. Your security will see a safe and perfect image of you. Now, call your lover and tell him to bring Sheila." He tossed a phone in my lap.

"No." My hands bound, I kicked at him, forcing a foot into his stomach.

He yanked my arms and pulled my body against his. His hot breath lingered on my neck. "Now, do as you are told and summon Ananiel."

Stormy. I screamed telepathically, hoping he'd react to our sigil connection.

David took a seat on the sofa and crossed his foot over his leg. "Seems you've banished my brother from the White House grounds, but no worries, I'll do the honors of filling your belly tonight. My seed will spoil the mating. Your prince will not desire you once you are branded as mine. Then I'll flaunt you in front of the American people as the filthy shifter you are. Your reputation soiled. The shifter nation destroyed."

"Stormy," I muttered. If this wasn't so tragic, I'd laugh at the irony, my reputation already exposed. The real horror was the kundalini. If I failed in preventing him from his defilement, then what happened didn't matter because all would be lost to the dark evil of society.

Ananiel whispered in my mind, *Fight!*

Gathering what energy, I could summon, I tapped into the color red and concentrated on the crystal candle sitting on the accent table beside a large flower arrangement. The candle rose an inch, but I couldn't get it to move. Losing my connection, the candle settled back on the table. David absorbed so much of my life-force. I lacked the ability to call on the gift of the gods.

Again, I tried, but this time the candle crashed to the floor, alerting David of my intentions. The fear choked a scream from my throat, my heart hammering in my chest. David pulled me from the floor and slammed me against the wall, knocking the remainder of my breath from my lungs. I grasped my chest.

He ripped the cotton shirt, exposing my breasts. He pulled my knife from the sheath tied around my calf and sliced my bra. Using the blade, he grazed the tip along my nipple and down my stomach.

The knife was sharp and if I moved or even took a breath, he'd slice me wide open. A sense of danger, fear, and helplessness assailed me. Determined not to let him witness my panic I never took my gaze from his.

"Haven't you figured out that Norman used you? Every step of your presidency, he was who prevented you from providing for the shifters. And now with the council, you've brought the alphas to us. The hunters will track them back to their territories," David said.

"Why?" The pain of realizing I could be responsbile for the destruction of the packs pierced me to the soul. My agony was so deep. I wanted to erect a wall around my heart and the pain Norm had caused.

"I'll show you." He slashed at my sweats.

I kneed him, trying to get him off me. Not tonight, not during the eclipse. *OMG, hurry, Ananiel.* The complete eclipse was in a few hours, and if this son-of-a-bitch raped and branded me, my mind would be forever tainted.

"I will have all of you. And the necromancer will keep you alive, never to return and find happiness in Elysium. When I take your soul, your powers will be mine."

His gaze scanned me with a look of defiant pleasure. His handsome features were a smile of pure sin, a smug, mocking smile.

With my hands pinned over my head, I couldn't reach my locket and touch the ancient magic. Alone, I wasn't strong enough, and that knowledge left me burning with rage at not expecting the use of the dark arts. I needed the cauldron's power. I wrestled my arms free from his grasp but still couldn't reach.

He slapped my cheek, breaking my concentration. "This is revenge for Sheila."

Caught off-guard, I stopped struggling and stared in bewilderment contemplating out what his sister had to do with the shifters.

I scooted back against the wall and raised my knees to my chest. Animosity hummed from him. "I've always been kind to Sheila...I cared for her. My family financed organization to support abuse victims like her."

"So naïve. I didn't want your money. I'll have revenge as payment for her life." The vengeance curled from his mouth like furious fire ready to scorch any who crossed its path.

"When I learned of you and your brothers, I had my perfect plan."

"How did you find out?" I pushed my body even harder against the wall, wishing it would open. I envisioned a portal behind me, but the energy sizzled out, not strong enough to break through the surrounding barriers.

His knees jammed my ribs, and he cupped my face in his hand. "I was just visiting the Red Rock Wildlife Refuge in Montana, where a Roger Isaeva was registered as a shifter with special permission to work along the boundaries of Yellowstone Park. With a little more investigation and I learned of your hybrid breeding."

His fingers dug into my skin the more he spoke of my family. "Let me go."

I closed my eyes and tried to ignore the ache that had settled just behind my heart. We hadn't been careful enough. I'd lived as a mortal, in secret to hide any connections to my mother's pack.

"Why do you blame the shifters? Or, better yet, me?"

"Shifters left Sheila to die. They destroyed her spirit, making her a shell of the witch she used to be."

Disgust rolled through me, and I didn't know what to say. If rogue shifters committed those crimes, they should be punished. "I'm sorry, David."

"You wouldn't listen when we tried to warn you. Then you forced the Senate to approve your civil rights act. No matter, I plan to taste the magic between your legs and leave you like they left Sheila. Then, I'll publicly denounce you before the Congressional Senate."

"No one will believe you." If the American public caught wind of the Saturnalia celebrations our females experienced before choosing their lifelong mates, the religious community would mark us as demons.

"Doesn't matter. I'll have stopped you from united the shifters."

His muscles grew taut against my hips. I had to keep him talking until Ananiel returned. "Why hurt innocent people over what one or two men did?"

"They destroyed her mind." He screeched in a soprano vibration, so close to losing control.

"The explosion today?" I asked cautiously but determined to find out.

"I've been planning it for weeks. Now, once I mate with you and destroy your lover, the shifters will have no leader and no protector."

Ananiel flashed into the room, his sword raised above his head. "No, don't kill him." I screamed.

The sword slashed through the air, embedding its blade into the Victorian chair on the other side of the coffee table.

In full regalia, his powerful reddish burned wings extended like a furious dragon's. Ananiel looked every bit the angel of wrath.

Unable to move, I watched from the floor, so happy to see him.

"Why should I allow him to live?" he bellowed giving me an exasperated look.

Now that David was off me, I regained my footing and confidence. "Some lines we can't uncross." My words reeled in his fury, but also to remind me of who I was. We were on the side of light, the side of the righteous, the side of justice.

"If he lives, he won't stop in his pursuit to destroy the shifters."

"He's a vicious vermin of the lowest kind, but killing him is wrong."

With his feet wide, his linothorax armor coverings, and his breastplate gleaming, he placed his hands on his hips looking every bit the Sarim prince of wrath. "I will disarm his defenses, making him vulnerable and unable to defend against his own magic. His enemies shall see him as weak, unable to lead the hunters. They will betray him for the scum he is."

"That works for me." I wrapped my arms around my knees. My blood temperature dropped, and I shook.

Ananiel rushed to my side. "Will you be all right?"

David rose from where Ananiel had tossed him and charged into us still holding my blade. Murder in his eyes. I screamed as the blade pierced my thigh. "Fuck." Still weak from the siphoning of my energy, I yanked the blade from my skin, and I let my 42 stiletto fly from my hand.

Ananiel caught the blade before it met its target. "No!"

"Get him out of here." The tremor in my voice must have alerted him to the seriousness of the situation. "Hurry, we have little time. The total eclipse is within the hour."

Ananiel lifted David into his arms and flashed from the room.

I shifted to heal, but something was wrong.

I called on the power of Apollo, the Greek god of healing. "Apollo, help me." My last gift from the gods.

Chapter Thirty-Four

GRACE

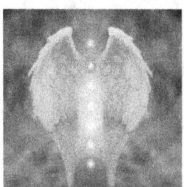

I writhed in discomfort, lying in a panicked frenzy curled on my bed. The precise moment of the shadow of the moon and sun grew close. The injury in my thigh burned, but the puncture wasn't life threatening but more a flesh wound. The real problem was the fledging pain in my womb. The intensity grew to an unbearable pressure. I became weaker with each passing minute. David left me drained and unable to use any of my gifts.

I glanced at the clock, three a.m. With the end of the total lunar eclipse, the early dawn would crest the Potomac River. We had little time, and Ananiel still hadn't returned. The witching hour, the time of death before the dawn of a new day approached.

A dark weave of gray magic spread through my womb, winding its way around my heart. "Norman, don't." The magic continued to move and surround my body to pull my legs apart.

"I'll claim you through gray magic."

I struggled against the spell. Getting on my hands and knees, I fought against his invasion. I wouldn't allow him to violate me, destroying the man I love. I would survive.

"Fight." I heard Apollo's voice in my head. Scrambling to concentrate my thoughts, I sought the strength of the sigil connection.

Images rose of Ananiel's beautiful red wings protecting me, shadowing me and loving me. My breath hitched as I watched him, a chilling certainty settling in my bones. A joyful laugh escaped my lips as I called out his name, his love a beacon, filling me with boundless hope and courage.

I clasped the locket around my neck. The color red filled my heart. A wrath stormed through me, and I pushed the gray weave from my body. Norman was on my mind and not here. He had no control if I didn't allow him access.

I am powerful. Red/orange hues grew, becoming so strong in their brightness. The room illuminated in its light, diminishing the grayness and bringing the light.

I shifted, and my silver wolf howled in her dominance over the dark. Healed, I returned to my human form.

Ananiel flashed into the room, taking me in his arms.

His fingers traced the delicate softness of my lower lip. "Next time, my love, it will be gentle."

We were frantic to complete the mating ceremony and to tie our souls together during the exact moment when the moon turned a sizzling red. Together, we shed our clothes, neither of us able to wait. "Take me home, my lover."

His beautiful, rigid cock slid inside my sleek, wet opening, his erection filled me, stripping away everything but my need.

My legs held him in a vise-grip. In a voracity of passion, every inch of my body was alive with savage energy. I sank my canines into his shoulder, and blood secured the sigil magic between us. Liquid fire singed my veins in a scorching wave of heat. Pleasure and release stormed through me, sealing our bodies. We grunted and gasped, locked in a mad embrace.

"My archeia," his voice husked my name as he pounded home, bursting into me and filling me with his seed.

****

Ananiel

I awoke with my body covering my lovely archeia. My brother, Uriel, established the root, the connection to the Earth and its elements. Moira, his archeia, would have the first baby born to the Sarim princes,

197

creating a new line of angels. I glanced over at my sleeping Grace; positive she'd conceived our young under the blood moon.

The trident gleamed on her thigh and I couldn't fight back the relief soaring through me. I kissed her and my hardened cock pushed against her warm flesh.

"Good morning warrior."

Grace's streaked hair fanned across her pillow. I couldn't help but admire the feisty beauty of my archeia. "You were brave last night."

"Together we completed our task. The sacral Carnelian scarab glows in the Svadhisthana chakra of the kundalini."

"Norman's magic was powerful; I almost lost to his mind manipulation."

"He'll never hurt you again. I promise." My grip tightened around her waist determined to keep her safe the rest of our lives.

She wrapped her arms around my neck and lowered me to her. "Now that we've completed the mating, in shifter society we're bound for life."

Her breath was warm and moist against my face, and my heart raced. My gaze was riveted on her face, then moved over her body slowly. A tingling in the pit of my stomach swelled to fill my spirit with an intensity I hadn't experienced in centuries. "Does that mean you'll become my wife."

"What about that first date?"

"I've just the place."

"Where?"

"Would you like to visit Kumuria?"

"The realm of the angels." Her eyes widened and a gleeful smile stretched across her face.

"I love you." Crushing her to me, I pressed my mouth to hers.

Also by Jaylee Austin

Good day peeps,

If you'd like to be part of my review or beta team, email me at https://jayleeauthor@jayleeaustin.com

Visit my website to receive insightful information about Jaylee's world. To enjoy a free book, join my mailing list visit https://linktr.ee/JayleesWorld

To help support me on my journey, join my exclusive Substack.

https://biancareeves.substack.com

Reviews are the lifeblood of an author. If you've enjoyed your reading experience, please leave a review.

I always enjoy hearing from you.

To all those readers who believe in the happily ever after, I write for you. A writer is powerful. We create people who are so real they break your heart. The world created by a writer becomes the dreams of other people. By the power of writing, monsters can transform into heroes and princesses into assassins.

Marvelous stories provoke emotions with their words, but it's the reader who falls in love with our world and shares a moment within our hearts.

Thank you for your support, your insight, and your commitment to reading a good story.

Monster in Moonlight Series

Labyrinth's Heart 2025

Coming Soon Book Two: Rex's Story

Cursed Connections: Coming out April 2026

New Monster Series

Satyr romances coming soon

The Return of the Draugr Series: Monster gothic romance

Shadows of the Harvest Moon

Shadows of the Yuletide 2026

Light of the Beltane Fires 2027

Light of Midsummer's Eve 2027

Christmas Magic Series

Heart Stone Magic

Contemporary Stand Alone

Dragonfly Heart

Valentine Angel-Novella

Sedona Series

Fairy Rose

Emerald's Cove

Agartha

Omnibus Set

Travel Through Time: All three books of the Sedona saga

Sarim Prince Series of the Archangel Universe

Magically Delicious

Storm Warrior

The Watcher's Guild

Bound by Destiny

Coming Soon Tattooed Justice in 2026

Omnibus Set

The Power of Love: The first three books

Spin-off series (Supernatural archangel Universe)

Yellowstone Wolf

Yellowstone Cougar

Coming soon Yellowstone Bear in 2026

Each of the books in The Sarim Prince and the spin-off series are books with their own romantic love story. But to have a perfect reader experience, I suggest reading the books in order to gain understanding of the universe in which the characters live. But it isn't necessary if reading for just the romance or adventure.

Book 1 Magically Delicious: Sarim prince series

Book 2 Storm Warrior: Sarim prince series

Book 2.5 Yellowstone Wolf: Archangel universe

Book 3 The Watcher's Guild: Sarim prince series

Book 3.5 Yellowstone Cougar: Archangel universe

Book 4 Bound By Destiny: Sarim prince series

Book 5 Tattooed Justice: Sarim prince series

Book 5.5 Yellowstone Bear: Archangel universe coming in 2027

Anthology and now released as a short story

The Spirit of Love: **A Timeless Curse** (Historical Time Travel)

The Light of Love: **The Snow Stag** (Historical Time Travel)

The Lure of Hunt: **Chasing Destiny** (A Sci-Fi Cyborg Romance)

Love Me in Vegas: Kickstarter/Author Nation: All or Nothing

About the Author

In a whimsical corner of the universe that echoes the enchanting realms of Wonderland, Jaylee Austin weaves tales that dance between the ethereal and the imaginative. Enthralled by mythology from every dimension—be it the enchanting Celtic goddesses, the vast treks through the nine worlds of the Nordic realms, or the ancient whispers of the Sumerian gods—she crafts modern romantic worlds that shimmer with magical realism.

Her desk, a canvas of creativity, is often interrupted by the playful pounces of her two adorable companions, but none more so than Tilly, her clever black pug. A true companion on her literary adventures, Tilly offers sage wisdom as they both ponder the mysterious questions that tug at the hearts of readers.

With a spirited background as a retired high school English and Theater teacher, Jaylee brought wit and warmth to the classroom, inspiring countless students to embrace their own creativity during National Writing Month. Through her enchanting stories, Jaylee invites readers to leap into alternate realities where the ordinary becomes extraordinary, and every page is a step further down the rabbit hole.

A city investigator tries to solve
a series of small-town shifter
crimes. One problem: the hot,
local alpha she needs to liaison
with is her ex

JAYLEE AUSTIN

YELLOWSTONE
WOLF 1